THE WARLORD, THE WARRIOR, THE WAR

THE RISE OF THE PENGUINS SAGA

STEVEN HAMMOND

ROCKHOPPER BOOKS

THE WARLORD, THE WARRIOR, THE WAR
Copyright © 2013 Steven Hammond
All rights reserved.
ISBN-10: 0615877451

ISBN-13: 978-0615877457 (RockhopperBooks)
2nd Edition

Edited by Michelle Patricia Browne
Cover art by Caner Inciucu
Interior layout by Tanya Adams

Exclusive content at:
http://riseofthepenguins.com/

Dedicated to

The lights that guide my day, Kirra and Charlotte

ACKNOWLEDGMENTS

I would like to thank everybody who helps me along this path. Kevin, Taylor, Melissa and Darrel for reading the rough version. Dan and Peggy for their wonderful support at A Book Barn. Joy for her never ending support and love. John for always taking the time to answer my questions. My editor, Michelle Browne for her hard work and helpful advice. The people who know more about these new-fangled computer gadgets than I do: Tanya, Jesse, Caner. The loyal few who keep me motivated. Abby, who thinks what I'm doing is awesome. Dino the cricket. Buster dog!

THE RISE OF THE PENGUINS SAGA

DRAMATIS PENGUINIS

General Talus, the Warlord of Planarseae—Royal Emperor

Cryzyrky—Adélie

Overlord Antaean—Royal Emperor

Supreme Commander Liutites—Royal Emperor

DRAMATIS PERSONAE

Trofim (Tro) Grekov—Mercenary (Russian)

Zachary Millerton—Mercenary (American)

Alyssa (A-Bomb) De Los Reyes—Mercenary (American)

Padre—Mercenary (Columbian)

Fabio (Fob)—Mercenary (American)

Colonel Tyler Jenson—U.S. military. Unknown branch.

THE WARLORD,
THE WARRIOR, THE WAR

THE WARLORD

CHAPTER 1

The warmer air of the approaching spring merging with the Antarctic ice shelf made the ice pop and snap. They could be heard all across the frozen plains. General Talus, Royal Emperor penguin and current commander of Forward Command One, stood motionless. He didn't yield even when the ice seemed to erupt beneath his feet. If he had any fear, whether of natural phenomenon or of man, he did not show it. Trepidation had been bred out of his bloodline two generations before he had been hatched.

The general was known as The Warlord of Planarseae, a region known to the humans as the Ronne Ice Shelf. He stood a full four feet tall, as tall as Supreme Commander Liutites, but without the Supreme Commander's bulk. The golden head feathers, common to Royal Emperors, extended outward and down majestically. His broad flipper wings tapered into fingerless grasping hands. Had his powerful jointed flippers not been designed for swimming they would have more resembled a human arm than a penguin's upper extremity. Scars decorated his body which he wore proudly as badges of victories against a long list of enemies, from Leopard Seals and other penguins to their hated human foes.

As an outcast from proper Royal Emperor society Talus delighted in committing raids against unauthorized targets, earning him a reputation as both a rogue and a stone in the Overlord's gullet. He and his army had achieved much, thought Talus with pleasure. He loved the mercenary life.

The Overlord had conceded Forward Command to him on the condition of its use to deal with problems that the highly structured Royal Emperor commanders could not. Talus was no fool. He knew that if the Overlord really wanted to put an end to his raids, he could do it in short order. Talus had only a hundred or so followers at any given time, usually the demented outcasts from other flocks, and the Overlord commanded thousands of penguins.

He hungered for more war. Talus himself was responsible for six human deaths in the first day of fighting. He remembered it with pride. During a fray on a Chinese research camp on a small island, Biochilles—the Royal Emperor regional commander—complained that Talus and those under his command were unnecessarily violent. The human remains were unusable for processing. The Warlord did not take kindly to the commander's criticisms. He carried Biochilles' head on the tip of his pike for a week. Rumor had it, Talus had used it to choke a Leopard Seal to death. Talus loved the way even his seasoned troops had looked at him after that incident.

Talus stood atop the rear wall of Forward Command, his articulated flipper holding his pike in a firm grip, watching Supreme Commander Liutites' contingent approach. Hatred surged in him at the sight of Liutites. Large, arrogant and powerful, the Supreme Commander of the Penguin Defense Alliance was second in command only to the Overlord.

He sized up Liutites. The favored son of Overlord Antaean seemed to have grown larger since they'd last crossed paths, nearly a year ago. Talus noticed fresh stains of blood adorning Liutites' breast, probably from some unfortunate underling who had delivered bad news. He considered ripping the Supreme Commander's throat out when he arrived. Talus ran his serrated tongue along the inside of his beak. The thought of fighting Liutites triggered chills of excitement. He ruffled his feathers at the thought.

That would be a battle for the ages.

"Supreme Commander Liutites," General Talus said, elegantly hopping off of the wall.

"Talus," Liutites said, barely suppressing his disdain for the rogue Royal Emperor. "As I am sure you are aware, elements of the PDA are attempting to secede from the Overlord's alliance. A Chinstrap of all things, Lavour, and a beakful of others have managed to take command of the entire PDA. It's spread our resources thin. But despite our depleted resources, the Overlord, in his mercy, has decided that this outpost requires fresh supplies."

"I should like to meet this Lavour. He sounds like someone who would fit in nicely with my collection of outcasts." Talus extended his flipper toward the mixed crowd of penguins meandering around the outpost. At the Warlord's mention, several of the penguins lifted their beaks up and let out a braying *whoop*. The calls echoed throughout the command post.

Liutites stared at the Warlord. He considered going for a quick kill and eliminating the problem of Talus once and for all. But he was under the strict orders of the Overlord not to kill him; they were spread too thin at the moment. Hopefully the oncoming threat of the humans would rid him of the nuisance. Liutites swallowed his desire.

"Perhaps you will, *General*. I see by the company you keep that you are most indiscriminate." Liutites had caught sight of a wanted criminal, a Gentoo penguin.

Talus caught Liutites' glare on the Gentoo. "These penguins are under *my* command and are subject to *my* protection. I suggest you turn your eye elsewhere, Supreme Commander."

The harsh Antarctic wind seemed to die as the two Royals stood with their eyes locked on one another's. Both Talus' and Liutites' warriors tensed in preparation for what seemed to be an inevitable clash. The Warlord's eyes narrowed. Liutites returned the look with a glint of pure, sadistic evil. They stood tense and unmoving, emitting guttural clicks of warning.

A sudden braying broke the tension. Both penguins relaxed.

"Saeson's aberrations have arrived," Liutites said.

Talus laughed. "If you and your Overlord would part with your prejudice, this war would already be over. Saeson's *aberrations,* as you call them, could easily tip the balance in favor of Antaean." The Warlord smiled inwardly when he caught sight of what was headed toward the outpost.

"Antaean also knows, as do you, what would happen if Saeson's brother, Aperion happened to be alive," Liutites interrupted.

"I do not fear the Basileios as you and your master do," Talus said, not flinching from the approaching convoy of Saeson's Misshapen. "Look at them—they are magnificent!"

"You know what could happen if the Basileios return in full."

"If you fear Aperion, hunt him down and kill him properly. You use too many words when you should be thinking of possibilities, Liutites. Close your beak and open your eyes." Talus gestured to the misshapen.

Liutites ignored him, walking away.

Talus too ignored the Supreme Commander. He focused on the procession of large penguins belly-sliding powerfully across the ice. Huge claws at what would be the elbow joint of the gull-shaped wings dug into the ice, while equally massive claws on the feet propelled the nearly ten-foot long penguins forward. Animal hide-wrapped rope tied across the creatures' shoulders and backs pulled a train of make-shift sleds containing weapons and other supplies. A Royal Emperor driver sat atop of the first sled, pulling reins attached to a crude bridle. A bit made of a human ulnar bone sat in the beast's spade-shaped beak.

General Talus could not help himself. As soon as the first behemoth came to a stop, he rushed forward to get a closer look. He inspected the glossy black plumage, pulling his articulated wing tip along the animal's body until he reached the head. Trickles of blood seeped from the corners of the creature's mouth. Talus met its deep black eye compassionately, sickened by the mistreatment of something so spectacular. He leaned in close to the prone bird and asked its name.

"It doesn't have a name. It is a Kauroch," Liutites said. Talus was so caught up in the beast that he hadn't noticed the Supreme Commander walk up from behind him. "It is a mindless beast of burden. Nothing more. They are all nearly blind, and useless as anything more than pack animals."

"Your prejudice will be your undoing, Liutites. Trust me on that," Talus said, inspecting the beast again. He saw a valuable resource, capable of thought and, if used properly, destruction.

"Your compassion for the rubbish will be yours," Liutites said evenly. "Mark my words, Talus. After this war is over, you will bow before me or you will die. It is only necessity which prevents me from killing you here and now."

"You aren't a necessity to me, Liutites. And I don't have a problem with killing *you* here and now."

In a flash of movement, Talus took Liutites' beak in his own and twisted his head, bringing him to the ground. Liutites was back on his feet in an instant. He struck Talus across the breast with his powerful flipper, sending the general to his back. The force of the blow surprised the Warlord. With Liutites bearing down on him, he had no time to think about the strike. The Supreme Commander lunged downward, hoping to strike the killing blow. Talus rolled out of the way, snatching his lost pike in the process.

Crowds of penguins moved in to watch the spectacle. None made a move to help their superiors, honoring their combat.

Liutites, undaunted, charged in close. It rendered the pike's sharp point useless. He beat the rogue mercilessly, driving Talus back until he was pressed against a Kauroch.

Talus weathered the assault, blocking most of blows with his pike. Feeling the firmness of the Kauroch's body to his back, Talus' eyes glinted with satisfaction. In one swift move, the Warlord swept the feet out from under Liutites with his pike. He brought the blunt end back to meet his skull. Liutites let out a grunt, but remained conscious. Talus brought his weapon up for the killing stab but his target rolled away and the deadly tip found only frozen ground. Talus howled in frustration and using his superior leg strength charged the Supreme Commander, knocking him back to the ground as he attempted to stand.

The two birds tumbled over one another. When they finally stopped rolling, they lay on their bellies, beak to beak. Hatred burned in their eyes. "I will enjoy ripping your heart from your chest," Liutites spat.

"Not as much as I shall enjoy liberating your body from its useless skull," Talus shot back.

The deciding blow was about to be struck when a bellow froze them. "Enough!"

Like boys caught by the principal in a schoolyard brawl, the two scrambled to their feet. The Overlord loomed, his sealskin cloak and Leopard Seal tooth necklace rustling in the wind.

"My Lord," Liutites said raising his beak, in a high salute.

Talus said nothing, only lifting his head in the most marginal of salutes.

"What is the meaning of this, Supreme Commander? I send you as an emissary to deliver supplies and you fight like fledglings over a fish?" Had it been another day, he would have let the two fight to the death. He knew the Supreme Commander had his eye on the dais of Overlord.

"My Lord, your *general* attacked me without provocation. I was merely ridding myself of a problem when you arrived."

"Is this true, General Talus?" Antaean asked, feigning surprise.

"I don't like him. I want to kill him," Talus said with a shrug.

Liutites growled quietly, looking as if he were about to strike again, The Overlord silenced him. "Our enemy is approaching. You may continue your dispute after the humans are vanquished. In fact, I look forward to it."

Talus stole a sideways glance at Liutites. "My lord," he said, "my scouts have sent word that a small detachment of the encroachers have broken off from the main group. They're headed in this direction, approximately one day out."

"That is precisely why I have sent you supplies, General Talus. I can get that information from a common Chinstrap. I hope you have something more useful to tell me," the Overlord said.

"If My Lordship would let me continue," Talus replied. He briefly entertained thrusting his pike through the bloated penguin's heart.

"You will address me as *My Lord*, General Talus. I will not remind you a second time," the Overlord rumbled.

Talus didn't waiver under the Overlord's icy glare, but he did think for a moment that he might have pushed the overfilled latrine of a penguin too far. "Yes, *My Lord.* I was going to say that your Kaurochs would be of great assistance to me here. They are magnificent creatures, and I could put them to a greater use than that of mere beasts of burden."

"And what use would that be, General?"

"They would augment my warriors, My Lord. Their speed matches the human vehicles."

"Our supply of these beasts is limited, Talus," Overlord Antaean said gesturing to the herd. He looked at Liutites and his eyes glimmered. "However, if you would pledge your loyalty to the Supreme Commander, so that I have your assurance that you will not attempt to kill him until the war's end, I might be able to part with two or three temporarily."

Talus recoiled at the thought, sneering. He looked at Liutites. He would never hold to such a bargain, but given the circumstances he would do what he felt necessary. "Of course, My Lord. We have a common enemy for the time being, and I will do what I must to assure our survival."

Liutites jerked in surprise. He thought Antaean's demands would put Talus over the top and that he would show his true colors—that of coward and a criminal. "What a pleasant turn of events, General. Perhaps in unity, we will turn the tides of this war," he said.

"Of course, Supreme Commander. However, once the war is over, we will resume our discussion," Talus said, resisting the urge to throw away the Overlord's gift and kill the smug bastard on the spot. He turned toward the Overlord. "My Lord. If I may, can I make use of one of the chariots?"

"Supreme Commander, see to it that three Kaurochs remain here. And make sure that one has a chariot. I am curious to see how the general makes use of them. Update him on the situation and return to Pack Ice Command immediately. We have much to discuss," the Overlord said. He returned to his Kauroch without saying another word.

Liutites lifted his beak in salute but quickly lowered it when saw that Antaean had dismissed him without as much as a glance. He resented being out in a Forward Command. He had much to discuss as well, but not with the Overlord.

Liutites turned his attention back to Talus. "The humans have already taken Forward Commands Three, Five and Six. Fortunately inclement weather has slowed their progress. After you successfully defend this command post, I will need you back at PIC."

"And what aren't you telling me? Pack Ice Command is well hidden. Why would you need me there?"

Liutites looked away and watched the Overlord as he departed. After a few more moments of silence, he turned back to Talus. "The Chinstrap has, in fact managed to take control of the PDA, even being so bold as to rename it the Alliance of Independent Colonies. They will, in all likelihood, attempt to overthrow our command. If you were to find the Chinstrap and kill him, the Overlord would see that you could move with liberty *and* allow you direct access to the Kaurochs."

"A bounty, then?" Talus said. "Very tempting, Supreme Commander. However, I'm sure Lavour has plenty of reasons to separate his affiliation with the alliance. You and your master's policies toward other clans have come back to bite you."

"The only thing that has come back to *bite* us, as you say, is the Overlord's dependency on the lesser clans. They are weak and lack the fortitude to bring the fight to the enemy," Liutites snapped back.

"How many Royals fought at the Falklands? I think you need to reassess your definition of fortitude. My experience has shown me that your so-called lesser clans have more than enough fight in them. You forget that I was at McMurdo. From what I saw there, I can see why you might be a little nervous at the prospect of penguins like Lavour returning to PIC with an army in tow." Talus smirked at Liutites, who could barely contain his rage. "In fact, I might just take you up on your offer and return to PIC after I kill these humans. I would dearly love to see how well you fare against a highly motivated Chinstrap. Wouldn't that be something? The mighty Liutites taken down by a lowly Chinstrap. And you know," Talus said quietly, "killing someone's entire colony may not be the best way to inspire loyalty."

Liutites gave a subtle jerk at hearing Talus mention the Chinstrap colony.

"Oh yes, Supreme Commander. I know all about you sending your stooge Diutes to do your dirty work. If Diutes was half the penguin he should be, he would have disobeyed and separated himself from the Penguin Defense Alliance, or maybe even associated himself with that hated resistance hiding in the shadows of PIC. You think you can act with impunity, that the Ancients have ordained your Overlord's rule. That all other clans should be subservient. A day will come when those who are forced into service will rise up, and your empire of miscreants will crumble."

Liutites quivered with rage. He fixed Talus with a glare icier than the surrounding landscape. Killing the Warlord would not be enough. He wanted to see him suffer and watch his self-confidence melt like a summer thaw.

"There will come a day when I become the Overlord and I will not suffer the likes of inferior penguins. And when that day comes, your impudence will be remembered."

Liutites turned his back on Talus and barked out orders to those unloading the supplies. He mounted a sled, staring at the Warlord as the Kauroch hauled him away.

CHAPTER 2

With the Supreme Commander finally out of the way, Talus could get on with more important things. He studied the Kaurochs for several minutes before calling on his aide. "Cryzyrky, what new information do you have for us? The Supreme Commander's update was somewhat dated."

Cryzyrky, an Adélie from the region known to the penguins as Cassokeesaw, or Marie Byrd Land, stood just over two-foot tall. She had lost a large chunk of her left flipper to a Leopard Seal and with it her ability to swim.

Cryzyrky approached Talus casually. "Well General, from the rumors I've heard, Diutes has been killed by the Rockhoppers on RHC 23."

"Well that's no surprise. Diutes had the cunning of an iceberg. What is a surprise is that he survived to maturity. And don't call me *general*," Talus said. Ever since he'd agreed to help Antaean and was given the rank of general, Cryzyrky had taken great pleasure in addressing him as such.

"Yes, General," she quipped . "There's more."

"Good or bad news?" Talus asked.

"Depends on your point of view. Apparently Colonel Kimmer was killed during the fight on RHC 23. I'm not sure how Kimmer ended up there, as he was slated for execution. I am assuming The Resistance had something to do with his escape. In addition, it seems that the Rockhoppers killed several of the Overlord's elite Shadow Warriors," Cryzyrky said, sounding impressed.

"Never upset a clan of Rockhoppers. They'll take it for a while, but once they set their mind to it, they fight like Ol' Cuasan himself," Talus said.

"Cuasan is a myth. I've never seen anything to make me believe that the Spirits of the Ancients guide us anywhere…especially Cuasan, the Prince of the Underworld," she said mockingly.

"All myth is founded in some truth, Cryzryky. Don't be so quick to dismiss the Ancients. After all, they led me to you," he said, chiding her on her lack of faith. "Now, back to what we *do* know."

Cryzyrky looked at Talus out of the corner of her eye. "Like Liutites said, the human advance has been stalled by bad weather. They are dependent on their machines, and it appears as if they don't operate very well during the storms of Huhellsus," she said, mocking the Ancient Spirit of Wind. "And there are two humans holed up in a structure—presumably the two that escaped from PIC. It's a three day trek from here, so it hardly seems worth the trouble."

Talus considered the information. "True. We have enough to deal with here. Perhaps we'll visit those two after we finish up." He paused and stared at Cryzyrky with a wry look in his eyes. "Huhellsus is with us. The Great Shaper has answered our request for help."

Cryzyrky looked at Talus doubtfully. "Do you really expect me to believe that the wind is a conscious being? And that the ocean, or so-called The Great Giver, controls the destiny of all living things? I'd have an easier time believing that a Gentoo is capable of rational thought."

Talus gave her a thoughtful look. "All I know, Cryzyrky, is that you and I are here only because of fortuitous events that neither of us had any control over. Whether that was because of the will of the Ancients or happenstance, I don't know. Like you, I don't have any proof as to whether the Ancient ones actually exist or *existed*. But I also don't have evidence to the contrary. I remind you that our paths crossed because there was a storm blowing in from the west and we turned to the east. And that was when I found you; starving and half-dead, but with a fire burning in yours eyes and a desire for something more. Whether that desire was for your own death or someone else's, I didn't know…and I still don't."

"I remember. My colony…lost to that windstorm…the Phocid. I will always be grateful that you took me when the Penguin Defense Alliance said I was too 'damaged'." Her eyes glinted with ferocity.

"I know what your name means in the Ancient language, *Unwanted*. You are anything than unwanted." Talus averted his eyes. "But that doesn't matter now. You've shown time and again that you are much more than you appear. So, again, whether it was blind chance or Huhellsus that crossed our paths, I don't know. I don't spend my days worrying about it either. Here we are. And that's all that matters."

It was as close that Talus would ever come to admitting he felt anything like kinship to another penguin. She looked at the battle-scarred warlord and promptly changed the subject. "So what's the plan? How are we going to kill these things once they arrive? Unless of course, Huhellsus sees fit to bury them in sheets of ice."

"The will of the Ancients notwithstanding, the Kaurochs will be instrumental. But first, we'll have to see how well they can dig."

THE WARRIOR

CHAPTER 3

Bald, muscular Trofim Grekov stared out the window of his crawler. The world outside spun around the motionless vehicle in a dizzying white maelstrom. He was not the type of man to easily lose his patience, but Lieutenant Zachery Millerton's decision to move out had cost the team precious resources, not the least of them being time. It had been a gamble. The storms in Antarctica were unpredictable, and the lieutenant had placed the wrong bet. Trofim, or Tro, as he was called by the rest of the mercenary team, grumbled a curse in Russian.

Colonel Tyler Jenson had assembled the team from special forces squads around the world. Trofim knew he wasn't really an officer in the U.S. Military, or probably wasn't, but he didn't care, either. Even being assigned squad leader and given the rank of sergeant meant little. Tro hoped that this mission would pay enough to be his last. He had been chasing phantoms, sometimes literally, in what seemed like every muck-pit, cave, or sewer on Earth for the past ten years. He was ready to give it over to the younger generation of mercs so he could retire to some quiet place on the west coast of America and spend his days watching baseball. Summer ball games and cool pines were a long way off from Antarctica, and Tro felt his patience ebb. He grumbled something to the man sitting beside him, threw on his hood, and exited the crawler.

The force of the wind pressed him against the vehicle. Undaunted, Tro lowered his head and trudged toward Lieutenant Millerton's crawler. The lieutenant's vehicle had the same tank-like treads as the others, but was twice the size of the other four in the convoy. He climbed up the ladder of the oversized crawler and banged on the door. After what felt like an inordinate amount of time, the door slid open and Tro fell inside.

"Where's your weapon?" Millerton demanded. Zachery Millerton was a large man, with dark skin and piercing eyes that spoke of his intelligence and intensity.

"I'm never unarmed," Tro said, removing his hood. Millerton sat back down at the two static filled monitors and communication devices of the command console.

"What can I do for you, Tro?"

"When are we moving out? We're wasting fuel and time."

"In case you haven't noticed, we're in white-out conditions. Colonel Jenson has strict protocols in place. We don't move in these conditions."

"To hell with the colonel. Since when has what a colonel said ever mattered to you, Zach?" Trofim snapped back.

"It usually doesn't. But this is different. This is a large scale operation, and we're not the only players on the field."

"I understand that, but we can't sit here indefinitely. These things are much more organized than anything we've seen before. What happened in the Falklands proves that. This is why I usually don't take American contracts. They like complete control, and see us as expendable." Tro sat in the chair next to Millerton and let out an irritated sigh.

"Why so tense? I've never seen you like this—not even in Columbia."

Trofim rotated his head in a circle, loosening the muscles in his neck. "I feel like we're bait. I don't like being the bait."

Millerton let out a laugh. "Columbia again? You weren't bait as much as you were a lure."

"Bait, lure, chum, it's all the same," Tro said, finally relaxing a little. "Tell me what do you know about Jenson. I didn't receive the pleasure to meet him."

"I've worked for him before. I don't like him, but the job pays well."

"You've worked for him recently?"

"Come on, Tro. You know the rules—clean up and shut up." Millerton shifted uncomfortably in his chair.

"This isn't the usual case of *clean up and shut up*. It's too big. A lot of people know about it. They can't just go in and make a village disappear or overmedicate some old fisherman. Thousands have been killed, and that can't be hidden," Tro said.

"You'd be surprised at what can be hidden." The lieutenant paused and looked away. "Over time, people forget, and the things that *are* remembered turn into legends or myth. Maybe even us, one day."

"It's hard to become a legend if you are anonymous," Trofim said. He spun around in his chair and stared out at the nothingness beyond the window. The clouds of blinding ice raced by, disappearing into the nothingness of white. Oh, he had made his mark in the world, whether it had been killing people while in the military or killing things that people would rather not know about. He tried not to think of this as his final mission. He refocused and thought of the job they were about to do. The job, as always, would involve killing, and killing was what he was good at. Besides, there were worse things than being anonymous.

"I will tell you this," Millerton said. "Jenson isn't much different than any of the others. You can't trust them; they have their own agenda. Just stay frosty."

"That's hard not to do here," Tro quipped. "But if he betrays us like that bastard in Columbia did, I won't hesitate to do a repeat performance."

Millerton laughed. "Still bitter about that, after all of this time? Remind me not to get on your bad side. I heard stories that pieces of that guy still fall from the sky every time it rains there. Boom! Man, that was a show." Millerton chuckled again.

Trofim stood and looked out the window once again. A break in the blowing ice allowed him to catch a glimpse of the blue sky. The puzzle piece of sky was as blue as he had ever seen. Then something else caught his eye. Something dark against an otherwise white landscape. He turned back to Millerton. "Are the satellite feeds up yet?"

"You're looking at 'em," the lieutenant said, indicating the static-filled screens.

Trofim swore and pulled a large knife from his under his coat.

"What are you doing?" Millerton asked. He stood and threw on his jacket.

"Staying frosty," Tro said. He threw open the door of the crawler and leapt to the hard-packed ice. He cursed at the pain of the landing. His knees weren't what they had been. He shook it off and headed toward what he had seen.

Tro approached a slope fifty meters from the crawlers and stopped to look around. He heard the faint voices of his comrades somewhere in the distance, but the wind masked their sounds. Surveying the surroundings, he couldn't see a thing. Still, his intuition told him he'd glimpsed a penguin. He squinted his eyes, hoping to make out a dark form against the white background, but the wind billowed with dusty ice. He looked back and realized he could no longer see the crawlers. Grasping his predicament, he sheathed his blade and slowly walked back towards them.

After a few steps, the wind nearly pushing him off of his feet, Trofim thought that he might have made a fatal error. The crawler was nowhere in sight, and he could hear nothing beyond the screaming wind. He swore again and strained his eyes to see. He didn't see the crawlers, but he did see the dark form standing just a few feet away. He drew his knife again and stepped toward the bird.

The penguin didn't move; it stood motionless, with its head down. Trofim put the knife under its beak and lifted the head. The penguin, which appeared to be a Chinstrap, looked at him with half-dead eyes. This thing was not a threat. Alone in the storm, the bird was freezing to death.

Tro wondered why it had come so close to the vehicles. He knelt down to get a better look at the hapless creature, still keeping his knife at the ready just in case. He knew what they were capable of.

The penguin opened its mouth and made a barely audible noise. "Help," the Chinstrap said.

Trofim jerked back in surprise. Was the wind playing tricks on him? If these things could speak, that changed the parameters of the mission. And if they did, why hadn't he been told? He knelt back in close, keeping his knife away. "Did you just ask me for help?"

The Chinstrap looked as if it were about to speak again when it heard Lieutenant Millerton's voice.

"Tro! There you are, what were you think—" Millerton spotted the penguin and drew his gun.

The Chinstrap looked at the lieutenant, then back at Trofim with imploring eyes.

Tro realized what was happening and began to stand. "No!" he shouted, as Millerton squeezed off two rounds.

The two-foot tall bird's body erupted into a spray of red mist and fell to the ground.

"What the hell are you doing?" Trofim yelled, swearing in both Russian and English. He looked at the dead penguin, then fixed Millerton with a hateful scowl.

Millerton threw up his hands in disbelief. "Have you forgotten the job? These things are the enemy. Seriously, what's gotten into you, Tro?" he casually holstered his weapon.

"Have you forgotten the protocols of BioCon? These *things* are intelligent, Zach. They talk. And part of those protocols state that if the biological entity is sentient and can communicate, then we must attempt to establish a rapport." Trofim's accent rumbled thickly with anger.

"I didn't know," Millerton said defensively. "Why are you crapping yourself over this? We've killed a hundred things without asking questions first."

"It was asking *me* for help, goddamnit," Tro said. He walked away.

Millerton motioned for one of the other soldiers. He had never seen Trofim act so volatile. He had seen others snap. The human psyche could handle only so many times facing death, and he wondered if perhaps his friend was nearing that point. "Keep an eye on him; we don't need any more wildcards thrown in our hand," he said, looking at the dead penguin.

CHAPTER 4

As he climbed inside the command vehicle, Millerton peered cautiously toward the console. He was surprised not to find Trofim. He sat down at the array and typed. The static-filled monitors sprung to life, each showing a thermally enhanced but distant view of tiny green forms against black. One screen showed what appeared to be a military CAMSS shelter, and the other, a mass of penguins. The door toward the back of the vehicle opened up. The lieutenant flinched. He reached for the keyboard, but thought better of it.

"My crawler doesn't have facilities," Tro said, as he ducked out of the tiny restroom.

"Being a commander has its benefits," Millerton said, spinning his seat toward Tro.

"Satellites up?" Trofim took the empty chair next to him. Millerton did not reply, keeping his eye on the feeds.

The silence settled for a few minutes. Millerton looked at Sergeant Grekov, who stared intently at the monitors. "Tro, I didn't know those things could talk, okay?"

"You heard me yell."

"Through that wind?"

"You fired with me in close proximity."

"I've shot targets off your back before. You don't trust my aim anymore?"

"I don't trust anyone or anything," Tro said, returning his gaze to the screen in front of him.

"Are you pissed? I said I don't ever want you pissed at me," Millerton joked, trying to ease the mood.

"The protocols? Do they still apply? If they don't, I didn't get the letter," Tro said. The image of the penguin's eyes looking to him for help just as it died haunted him. There was something more to this. Those eyes… There was intelligence and emotion behind them. And why was it out there alone? What was it running from?

Tro shook his head. Why did it have to be running from something? It had probably just gotten lost. Animals and people got lost all of the time.

"It's memo," Millerton said, pulling Tro out of his thoughts.

"Huh?" Tro asked.

"It's *memo*, not letter. You'd think after speaking English for twenty years you could get the expressions right," Millerton jibed.

"Memo, letter—same thing," Tro said, allowing his Russian accent to thicken. He looked at the screens and tapped them both. "Where are these?"

"This one is near your friends at Progress," he said, pointing to the first screen, "and I'm not sure of the second. It looks like a temporary military compound. Why there are penguins there, I don't know. I do know that the first encounters have been a success," Millerton said.

"Bullets and explosives usually mean success against soft targets," Tro said, still thinking about the Chinstrap. "There's not many there. Can you zoom in?"

Millerton tapped a few keys. "I don't think so—I don't have much control of what we see."

"Is this the compound that they operate from?" Tro asked, pointing at the first monitor.

"I doubt it. The last I heard they had some colonel named Maycotte taking care of that, but he's still in the States."

Trofim studied the monitors and noticed a strange thing; all of the penguins quickly departed from the unknown location on screen two. "It looks like they left," he said.

"Hm," Millerton said, no longer paying attention. He was looking out the window, watching the landscape come back into view. The wind had died down as suddenly as it began. "Better get your crew up. We'll probably be moving out soon."

Tro remained sitting. "After this is over, we're going to discuss the protocols more. I want to know why the BioCon rules no longer matter. If you ask me, this mission is starting to give me a bad smell in my mouth."

"I think you meant taste," Millerton chortled. "Tro, we've already been through this. Protocols aside, this isn't a pursue and capture situation—you heard the briefing—this is an exterminate with extreme prejudice event. We were hired to do a job for a particular entity, and we have to conform to the parameters set by that entity." He leaned back and waited for a reply. When no reply came he leaned back and studied Tro. "Christ, you're pissed at me. You're gonna blow me all to hell like you did Vargas, aren't you?"

Tro had to chuckle. "Only if you use me as bait."

Millerton smiled. "I can't make any promises."

"Then neither can I," Tro said. As he stood, he pointed to the second monitor. "Somebody's waving at you."

Millerton looked at the screen. A small thermally-enhanced man was waving his arms frantically outside of the CAMSS shelter. The image flashed bright white from a detonation and the feed abruptly cut off. Tro and Millerton looked at each other. "Bad taste or smell, I'm beginning not to like this," Trofim said.

CHAPTER 5

By the time Tro got back to his crawler, the brief daylight had already passed. Colonel Jenson decided that they should travel to within five kilometers of the designated target and await further instructions. This news did nothing to ease the sergeant's already upset mood. He felt there was something Zach Millerton was not telling him. The way Zach had acted when he came from the restroom told him enough. But Tro also knew that that was the nature of this kind of work—most information was on a need to know basis, and apparently *Lieutenant* Zachary Millerton felt that *Sergeant* Trofim Grekov did not need to know. In most cases, that was fine with Tro. After witnessing what he had via the satellite feed, not knowing was not good enough for him. Added to that were the broken protocols of the Biological Containment Unit, a confederation of special-forces teams often called upon by various governments and corporations to deal with biological entities that shouldn't exist.

The air had gone foul. Trofim was not sure whether he would survive this frozen hell long enough to sit on a porch and sip kvass while listening to a ball game on the radio. He wanted nothing more than to turn his crawler around, drive it straight up the ass of whoever was calling the shots on this mission, and resign. But he needed the big payday to see his dreams come to fruition. So, instead, he pushed the thoughts from his mind and meditated, like he had before almost every assignment since before he joined the B.C.U.

During his meditations, Tro saw the Chinstrap's pleading eyes once more. He heard the barely audible word, beseeching him for help. His mind floated on the waves of his meditative state and traveled back to a place he longed to forget.

An arid region, dust swirling in the choking heat. He looked through his younger eyes and saw shadowy forms fleeing a burning building. The flames seemed to reach for those who tried to escape, only to pull them back into the Devil-stoked furnace. The screams of the victims ceased as the fire tore the cries from their lungs.

He saw it, the quarry they had spent the past week searching for. An unnaturally dark shadow in the center of the conflagration, impossibly white eyes staring back at him through the doorway of what had once been an adobe lodge. Each time before, they had come close, arriving just too late, but not this time. What they had come to call, the Djinn was real. As with most real things, they could be made unreal with a bullet. Trofim felt his younger self raise his weapon and put the fabled being firmly in his sights. Then he felt himself being drawn in, as if he could feel the Djinn's thoughts: fear. In the instant before he pulled the trigger, he also felt what it had wanted. Help. The shock of the Djinn's touch on his mind made him pull the trigger. The bullet sliced through the super-heated air. The white eyes opened wide, not in horror, but in questioning disappointment.

The vivid memory jarred Trofim from his meditation. He let out a deep breath and sat staring at the Aurora Australis, dancing in ribbons of red and green light across the night sky. His thoughts reminded him that he had abandoned the protocols back then and tried to excuse his actions by the same means Millerton had on this day. Trofim believed that there was a reason behind every action, and he wanted to know the reason behind the Chinstrap's. If Millerton knew and wasn't telling him, well…Columbia was going to look like a firecracker by comparison. Mesmerized by nature's display of charged particle beauty, Trofim drifted into a shallow sleep.

His eyes opened just before the rap on the window came. A haze of potential sunlight drifted across the sky, heralding the end of the darkness. Tro threw the door open, feeling the icy blast of the Antarctic air. It instantly sharpened his senses and brought the slumbering men from their dreams and nightmares. "Good morning, Alyssa. I take it we're *finally* ready to get this maneuver underway?" he asked, knowing full well that they were.

Alyssa De Los Reyes. Her name was as much a dichotomy in heritage as was her appearance was a juxtaposition to her combat abilities. Young, auburn haired, she had a fair complexion and eyes that sparkled with merriment. It seemed impossible that a sweet person like her could be the same intense, violent force of nature who'd earned the moniker 'A-Bomb'.

"Good morning to you too, Tro-tro. Move over, I'm freezing my ass out here," she said, giving Tro a shove and throwing her gear on his lap.

"Tro-tro? Is that your best today?" he asked, amused.

"Do you know how hard it is to come up with a cutesy name for somebody named Trofim?"

"There are plenty of ways in Russian that I could tell you, but then I'd have to kill you," Tro said, making room for her.

Alyssa raised an eyebrow doubtfully. "Easier said than done, pookie-cakes."

"That's just awful. Pookie-cakes? That sounds like something you'd find in the latrine."

"Then it looks like I finally found you a name that fits. And yes, we'll be moving out shortly. Millerton said I should ride with you," she said, raising her eyebrows.

"Keeping eyes on me, then? He's afraid of explosions, you know."

"From what I heard, I should be too. And they call *me* A-Bomb?" Alyssa scooted in next to Tro, drawing the protest of the man sitting on the other side. "Make room, Padre. Ladies first."

"The Bible tells us women should be subordinate to men." Padre grumbled. The Hispanic man had gotten his nick-name from his frequent

Biblical references.

"It also says *thou shalt not kill*, and yet here you are—fully armed," she said, without looking at him.

"It tells us that we have dominion over all living things... and the killing part refers to people. Present company excluded, we don't usually kill people," Padre retorted.

"That's enough," Trofim said. "Let's start the party. Who am I following in?"

"Yeah! Let's start the party," Alyssa laughed. "Martin's crew is taking lead. Stay close behind. Millerton said we aren't sure what kind of resistance we'll be facing—the satellite feed has been blacked out for some reason. Maybe somebody doesn't want this to be broadcast."

"I don't know if that's a good or bad thing," Tro said, thinking about what he had seen earlier. It was just as well—he didn't like being watched while he worked, especially if those doing the watching controlled the missiles. He glanced at Alyssa when the crawler started moving. "Are you ready?"

"The A-Bomb is primed and ready to detonate," she replied, terrifyingly giddy.

THE WAR

CHAPTER 6

"Cryzyrky, tell those Gentoo to quit dawdling and get out of the trenches," Talus said. He stood atop of the northern wall of Forward Command and surveyed the work in the dim morning light. The one hundred plus penguins under Talus' command worked well into the night. After huddling together for the night to stave off freezing to death, the Warlord dispersed the group to make the final preparations for the eminent encounter with the humans. "And make sure the seal-holes are reopened. They are essential to this plan."

"Yes, sir," Cryzyrky said, drawing a stern but not entirely serious look from Talus. "The Kaurochs have completed their work. The trenches have been widened, but if you don't mind me saying, I don't see what good that will do. Their vehicles can easily traverse them."

"If all goes well, they'll be on foot. The trenches are there only to slow them down. Just remember the plan. And don't forget, Cryzyrky—when I say get to the chariot, don't hesitate. If we are to defeat these men, we have to do everything as I laid it out. A single human weapon has enough power to kill every one of us, and I'm certain all of them will carry more than one."

Cryzyrky looked to the brightening sky. "This will be your greatest victory. I doubt the humans are prepared for what you have planned," she said, trying to bolster her own confidence. She knew of the PDA's previous encounters with humans. Even with far superior numbers, the Alliance had taken massive casualties. Regardless of what Talus' plans were, if it came down to him dying during combat, she would go to The Great Sea with him. He had given her purpose and life, and she would die by his side if need be.

Talus hopped down a set of stairs and surveyed the courtyard of Forward Command. Two-meter high walls surrounded an area of approximately twenty-thousand square feet. Jagged ice jutted to the left and right of the compound, stretched out for nearly a mile in either direction. Talus shook his head. "I don't like being boxed in like this. If truth be told, I would like to meet the designer of this layout and skewer him with my pike from head to tail for the stupidity of it."

"Are there any other options?"

"If the Overlord had not been so stingy with the Kaurochs, there would have been," Talus said, looking at the sky as it grew brighter.

Tremors from beneath the ice rattled their feet. A steady scraping near the seal holes drew the attention of every penguin within the command post. The ice began to crumble into the sea around the holes. A large black head surfaced, took a breath, and continued to scrape at the edges with its spade-like beak. Where there were once several holes, there was now one. The head submerged, and within seconds, the Kauroch sprang from sea. Its gargantuan body slid to a stop with grace and ease in the center of Forward Command. Within moments, another Kauroch emerged, repeating its predecessor's grace.

Talus' eyes glinted with pride and satisfaction as he approached the Kaurochs. He gently rubbed his flipper along the faces of the beasts as he strode by, looking at them with the admiration of a father seeing his son come of age.

The Kaurochs issued soft groans as Talus spoke to them in a quiet voice that only the beasts could hear. He stepped back and the Kaurochs raised their heads, as if awaiting more kind words. Talus lowered his head and both creatures slid back into the sea.

"Cryzyrky, the Kaurochs have informed me the humans are on the move. Call the warriors to arms…the fight has come to us." He climbed back up the parapet.

Cryzyrky sounded the alert, and those who could bear weapons selected spears with tips made of teeth or scavenged metal, fixed with the sinew of past victims. Those without the grasping hands of the Royals bore only the ferocity of their will. Royal Emperors, Gentoo, Adélie, Chinstraps, King and Rockhopper stood side-by-side awaiting the Warlord's instructions. With the combatants assembled, Cryzyrky ducked into an alcove in the back wall used as a food store.

Talus stared into the horizon; he couldn't see the humans, but they were there. His heart beat with the thrill of death. It had been too long since his last kill; even the battle with Liutites hadn't been enough to quell his inner rage. His tongue quivered in his beak with anticipation, and he turned toward the congregation, all of whom saw the familiar gleam of impending violence in his eyes.

Talus studied each of them, over one-hundred strong and each eager for battle. "Those of you who have been with me for any span of time know that I am not one to give speeches before a fight. You know what is expected of you and you know what to expect from me. But today we face a foe much more prepared than anything we have faced before. The raids and skirmishes we have been through will pale in comparison to this day. The outcome is uncertain. Many of us will likely die in battle. I wish it were otherwise, but that is the reality. We do not fight for the Penguin Defense Alliance or the Overlord; we fight because that is what we were born to do. We are mayhem, we are chaos and we are fear. The plan is set. You know what is expected of you, and if we die in combat, may the Ancients guide us on our journey to The Great Sea." He searched the crowd for Cryzyrky until he spotted her. She was emerging from the alcove, dragging a curious item. "Now, we wait. Assume your positions and rest while you can."

Talus climbed off the wall and met Cryzyrky in the center of the compound. Looking down at the diminutive Adélie and her cargo, he couldn't help but be intrigued. "Well, what did you find in the food stores? I don't seem to remember skins being on the menu."

Cryzyrky looked at her commander with reproach in her eyes. She dropped her parcel and quickly unfurled it on the ice. As she did, a long wooden object rolled out. "This is not to eat, Your Warlordfulship. This is my gift to you." She presented him with a tunic made of seal-leather.

Light-gray, with the seams roughly sewn together by thin strands of dried tendon, the garment had considerable mass to it. A harness of thicker leather, which lay on top, added to the weight. But what caught the Warlord's eye was the wooden object. Three-foot long, with a tapered handle carved to fit the grip of Talus' articulated hands. It had edges as perfectly square as anything Talus ever seen. He quickly snatched it up, feeling the heft of it in his hand. He admired the weapon, imagining the damage that could be done to a human skull with such a thing. "Where did you find such a weapon?" he asked Cryzryky.

"You approve?"

"Yes. Yes," he said, swinging the weapon from side to side. "But how? How did you come across this?"

Cryzyrky lifted her head in with pride. "I have connections with the Imperial weapon maker. I sent a message when I found out you were taking this post. I feared it wouldn't arrive in time, but to my relief it did. He smuggled it in the delivery."

"Oh if I had this when Liutites was here. I would have loved to have cleaved his skull and shut his worthless beak for good," Talus said. He looked at Cryzyrky with admiration. "You are a remarkable penguin. You never fail to amaze me. If there is one penguin that I have ever called my friend, then you are that penguin. Thank you."

He quickly returned his attention to the club. It was well balanced and made of wood, not bone as one would expect. Wood was a precious commodity in Antarctica; this was likely scavenged from an abandoned whaling station. His gaze shifted from the weapon to the leather. "And what, I bid the Ancients, is this?"

Cryzyrky was humbled by the Warlord's appreciation, but didn't dare say a word about the unusual praise. "This is made of seal-leather, thick for added protection." Talus was about to object. "And it has a holster for your weapon," she added quickly.

Talus considered the gift. Looking like the Overlord was a small price to pay to carry two weapons. His pike was great for striking an enemy at a distance, but as his fray with Liutites proved, a close quarters weapon would be very useful. "How do I put it on?"

"Treocles," Cryzyrky called to a nearby Royal Emperor. "Come and assist the Warlord with his armor."

The Royal lifted the garment easily, wisely not commenting on the Warlord needing armor. "Spread out your flippers," Cryzyrky said, running from the front of Talus to his back. "Now lower you head." The Royal slid the vest on Talus while Cryzyrky tugged at the bottom with her beak. The harness which supported the holster was next. Cryzyrky told Talus to take a deep breath as she cinched up the sinew straps.

Talus barely felt the weight of the leather, his body being supported by stout and powerful legs. He slid his new weapon neatly in the holster, which slung across the right side of his body. He pulled the club out a few times to get the feel of the motion. He grabbed his pike and practiced a few thrusts to see if the get up hindered his motion. Satisfied, he turned to the Adélie and dismissed the Royal. He was about to speak, but stopped and cocked his head, listening. An emperor penguin's call can be heard from a kilometer away, but the Kauroch's call could be heard from an even greater distance. As Talus listened to the report, the familiar bloodlust returned to his eyes. "The humans are near. Be ready."

CHAPTER 7

Five crawlers and the command vehicle: twenty-eight soldiers. They moved across the ice with haste, rattling the occupants as they hit ruts and moguls. The constant shaking did little to put the soldiers at ease. Despite protests, the drivers maintained their speed. Daylight was breaking, and they would have precious little time to get in, clean up, and move on before the darkness returned. The plan was simple: wipe out the defenders and get back to the ship. Barring any more windstorms, they expected to be back within a few hours.

Trofim and A-Bomb relaxed as best they could, discussing whose baseball team had the best chance of going to the series.

"Damn it!" a voice yelped as they hit a particularly nasty bump.

Trofim looked to rear seat. "That's not proper language coming from a priest," he said with a smile.

"I'm not a priest. And I was merely asking God to damn these bumps to hell," Padre retorted, his voice rattling from the rough travel.

"And speaking of sending something to hell, why didn't they just send a cruise missile and blast the living crap out these things instead of sending us in?" A-Bomb grunted. "God *damn* it, can you ease up just a little, Fabio? We're all gonna be exhausted by the time we get there."

The driver, nick-named Fabio for his ever-present tan, long hair and brilliant white teeth, flashed a dazzling smile at her. "No can do. I'm trying to keep up with Martin's crew," he said, referring to the crawler leading the group. He purposely swerved the crawler toward a nasty rut, drawing more groans of complaint.

"And for Christ's sake, close your mouth. We'll all go snow-blind before we hit the ice," A-Bomb snapped.

"I got the standard answer when I asked that same thing," Tro shot back. He gave Fabio a withering glare for purposely hitting the rut. "Boots on the ground. Gather intel; we have something special planned for them later. The same BS we always get. But I get the feeling that these command posts are not the real target. They're after something bigger."

It was close to the same thing he had heard a hundred times before. And it was one of the reasons why Tro wanted out of the game. It was the super-secret, cover-up nonsense that got to him. You never knew who to trust. While it was true that most of the time you could have faith in your squad mates, and really, you had to, when things went to hell, you just couldn't trust the leadership.

Tro was getting that same feeling of mistrust with Millerton. Even though they had been through the maelstroms together, sometimes literally, there was definitely something different about him this time. Maybe Millerton was getting tired of the game too, and had finally sold out to the powers that be. Maybe he'd gotten a bad case of ambition. Whatever it was, Tro decided that he would find out as soon as this mission was over. And if Millerton ended up selling them out, he always had plan B.

A-Bomb looked at Tro, and he studied her face to see what she had to say. How someone with eyes that seemed to be in a state of perpetual delight could have the skill in combat and her capacity for pure violence never ceased to amaze him. There was never a hint of some past trauma or underlying psychosis in her eyes that seemed to lead others into the life of a mercenary. There was only the joy of the work she did. Behind those eyes lay intelligence. It was the cunning to handle almost any situation, knowing when to kill and when not to kill. And the latter was what made

Tro respect her more than any man he had fought beside.

"Is this really going to be your final assignment?" she finally asked.

Trofim hesitated. "I prefer not to say. Superstitions and all."

"Well if it is…it's been a pleasure," she said. The two looked at each other. Both had an equal amount of respect for the other. "Maybe I'll call it a day too, and spend my evenings sitting at the ballpark, screaming at the umps."

Alyssa looked away and Tro saw what could be a glint of sadness in her expression. The look caught him unprepared. "You're spooking me, lady. Besides, this isn't a one mission assignment. We might be here for an intermible, intermittibly—"

"Just say a long time," Alyssa said, sparing him the trouble of saying interminably. The two shared a laugh at Tro's expense.

Hearing the conversation, Fob leaned in close to Trofim. "Hey, I think she got a thing for you. You want me to park this so you two can have some alone time?"

Trofim glanced at Alyssa, who looked as if she were about to say something. In the next instant, Trofim's knife was unsheathed and the edge of the blade pressed against Fabio's mouth in the time it took to blink. He leaned in close to the driver and spoke slow and quiet. "I don't need a chauffeur on this trip. If I hear one more comment like that, I'll cut your jaw from your head to make certain you won't say it again." As if having an eight-inch blade pressed against his mouth wasn't enough, Trofim's Russian accent punctuated the threat.

Fabio nodded slowly. He had no doubt that Trofim meant every word of what he had said. "Sorry," Fob said, being careful not to move his tongue against the blade's edge. "I didn't mean to piss you off. Just joking," he continued, after the knife moved away.

"Oh, that wasn't pissed," Alyssa said with a smile. "That was barely annoyed. I shudder to think what a *pissed* Grekov would be like."

"There it is," Trofim said giving Alyssa a sideways smile. He pointed to a ridge in the distance that marked their target.

"Are you sure?" Padre asked from the back.

"Yes. That's not a natural formation. To the left and right, yes, but not the middle," Tro answered. As confirmation to his assessment: his earpiece crackled to life.

"This is the place, about a half a klick dead ahead," Millerton's voice confirmed. "Gear up and stay alert. We are going in hard and fast, and see if we can't mop this up in a half hour."

As the squad got to the work of checking weapons and gear, Trofim gave them one final reminder of the plan. "This is a boots running operation. We open the doors; we haul ass, infiltrate and kill. Eddie's squad will lead, followed by us. A-Bomb, since the Lieutenant saw fit that you accompany me on this ride, you're now in my squad. Trader's and Hory's squad will follow us in, and Millerton's group will stay in reserve. As you know, these aren't the cute penguins you see in cartoons. They are dangerous and they are intelligent. They've already killed thousands here, and in the Falklands, and other places. Any questions?" Tro asked, looking each member in the eyes to check their nerve.

"Yeah, just one?" asked the youngest member of the team. It was Dik-dik, who'd earned the embarrassing moniker after getting spooked during a maneuver in South Africa and killing one of the tiny antelopes. "If these things have killed thousands, how are less than thirty of us going to take them out?"

"The penguins had the advantage of surprise and they numbered in the millions against civilian populations. We are trained killers, and there are only one hundred or so that we know of at this location. It shouldn't be problem. Now let's—"

"Shit," Fob shouted. "Hold on!" The driver hit the brakes of the crawler hard, tossing the occupants from their seats.

"What happened?" Tro yelled. He was on his feet before he finished the question.

"Eddie's crawler fell through the ice," Fob said. He threw open the door and started running toward the hole.

"Everybody out! Move, move, move," Tro ordered. The squad leapt from the vehicle with weapons ready. They sprinted to the where the lead crawler had disappeared.

"Stand back," Tro said. They reached the hole in the ice. He searched for any movement in the water. Fractured ice bobbed on the surface and water quietly lapped against the edge. Nothing else. Not even a bubble.

"Get a winch. Maybe we can hook them," Padre said. He turned toward the squad from another crawler.

"Forget it," Millerton said having just arrived. "This water is deep... and cold, around four degrees Celsius. Even if they got out, they'd be dead within minutes in that water."

"I thought you said the ice was thick? That doesn't look very thick to me," Fob yelled.

"The conditions change here day by day—hell, sometimes hour by hour. Our intel said the ice floes were thick enough," Millerton snapped back.

"Well now we see how good your intel was—"

"They didn't break through. This hole was dug," Trofim said. He inspected the area for fissures and other tell-tale signs of stress fractured ice. There were none. Then he noticed what appeared to be grooves dug into the bottom of an overturned piece of ice, floating on the surface and along the edge. He let his eyes rest on Millerton. What they were dealing were either much more advanced than what he had been told, or they had help. Human help. "What do you know that you're not telling us?"

Millerton threw up his hands. "Tro, it's a hole in the ice. If it was dug, then it was probably dug by these things. They're smart, we both know that. We've been over this. We just lost six good soldiers. Now, I'd suggest you focus on here and now, and get over your trust issues."

Trofim took a deep breath. The icy air burned in his lungs, but it helped cool his thoughts. Maybe Millerton was telling the truth, or maybe he wasn't.

Their opponents were intelligent, hell, they could talk; they were highly organized, and they had a penchant for violence that was surpassed only by man. "Did the other teams run into anything like this? Traps?" he asked, surveying the surroundings. He looked toward the command post in the distance. He had a feeling…no, he *knew*, they were being watched.

Millerton answered, but Trofim was already giving his squad orders. As expected, the answer was *no,* and he didn't need to hear the extended version.

"A-Bomb, Parker, Dik-dik, spread out and see if there any signs of more traps. Stay awake—we don't know what else is in store for us. Padre, see if we have anything to mark the other holes."

"What makes you think there are more?" Padre asked.

"If you were setting a trap for an enemy, would you set just one?"

Padre gave a sideways nod and ran back to the crawler.

The remaining squads followed Trofim's lead and fanned out across the frozen surface. The sun was rising ever higher in the vivid blue sky, creating a glare which made the search for traps that much more frustrating. Time was essential—the plan was to be in and out in the span of the abbreviated three-and-a-half hour day; less, if possible. Not long after the men and women began their search, they started calling out, finding more places where the ice appeared to be slightly more translucent, as if it had been scraped thin. By the time they finished their work, they had found a total of twenty one areas where there appeared to be traps.

"It appears as if the bulk of the holes are dug out to the south-east," Padre reported to Trofim and Millerton. "If we head west, we should be able to circumnavigate them."

"I wonder why they are more concentrated in one area," said the lieutenant.

"Probably ran out of time. It would have made more sense to just surround the compound," Padre said.

Trofim studied Forward Command through binoculars he borrowed from Millerton, while the others debated why the holes were dug and where. It seemed strangely devoid of movement. Not a single penguin could be seen. If they were expecting an attack, then surely they would have sentries or patrols. Tro pondered the traps and lack of movement. "They want us to go that way," he said.

"Huh?" the two others said in unison.

"It's a kill zone. They are funneling us in. They probably have more surprises. I suggest we go on foot from here."

"No," Millerton said, too quick for Trofim's taste. "We need the equipment in the crawlers."

Trofim studied the man, but decided to put his growing distrust aside. "Then we move slow—three men on foot leading the way."

"That'll take time."

"We aren't surprising anyone. They know we are here," Tro said. He didn't like sending the men on foot, but it was the only way to assure they wouldn't fall into another hole. He figured the scouts would be safe enough. Unless, of course, the penguins had artillery, and he was relatively certain they didn't have that kind of technology. Millerton agreed.

Trofim barked out orders and watched as everyone returned to their respective vehicles. With the scouts in position, Trofim turned to go back to his crawler, but Millerton stopped him. "Does this mean you're going to tell me what the hell is going on now?" Tro asked.

"This was supposed to be an easy-in easy-out operation. But when do we ever get that?" Millerton said. He paused and surveyed the landscape. Trofim followed the lieutenant's gaze. Brilliant white as far as the eye could see, with violet mountains in the distance of the otherwise sparse scenery. The sky was as blue as anything he had ever seen—almost unnaturally blue. As if he gazed upon it for too long, it would swallow him and take him someplace unknown. He thought about it. Yeah, he was getting tired of this, tired of the killing, and just tired overall. He thought about what Alyssa had said, and watching a ballgame with a friend sounded pretty good about now. Really good in fact.

"Okay, here's the *more* you've been so worried about," Millerton said, once the others were out of ear-shot. "What we're doing here will fundamentally change the world. With the American military on the ground, all of the Antarctic treaties and protocols have been broken. Technically, we're in French territory, but the Americans will claim it as theirs. And I doubt that France would be willing to go to war against an ally as powerful as the U.S., so the territory will likely be conceded."

"We're conquerors now?" Trofim asked. He was definitely starting to get a very bad *smell* in his mouth. This was another reason why he hated taking jobs for the Americans; there was always something else.

"So to speak," Millerton said. "But that's not all."

Trofim looked at him. "I never doubted that."

"These outposts, as you know, are a perimeter. They're here to protect whatever or whoever is controlling these things. And we don't know where that is exactly. There is one person who does, a guy named Lyons or something, but he's not being cooperative," Millerton paused again. "Didn't you wonder about this unusually large paycheck we're getting?"

"You know me. I don't ask questions...unless I feel like I'm being used as bait. But it's too late to turn the job down now, isn't it?" Trofim said. He was getting frustrated. When he took the job, he thought it was just a case of local fauna gone wild. Then he learned the truth—the Falklands. And then he was told about South Georgia. Even though the human population there was sparse, it didn't take away from the fact that nearly a hundred men and women had died there. Then to learn they could communicate, not just gestural communication, but actually speak. He wondered if they had been genetically altered, like so many other cases he had dealt with, but that wasn't the truth either. They were just smart—human smart.

"Here's what I know. A branch of the American government is working with Global Technologies or Global Threat, or whatever they're calling themselves these days, and this whole thing was set up. Well, Antarctica was anyways. They knew the penguins were intelligent and they manipulated them. But things didn't work out how they had planned…obviously. Things got out of control. They were just supposed to give the Americans a reason to come to Antarctica and establish a military presence, which, and I'm only surmising this, would leave the door open for mining and drilling rights. Add to that, there are at least two previously unknown species involved. And they are after one in particular. I haven't been briefed on that part and I only overheard Colonel Jenson mention it briefly to somebody named Turlock. So the short of it is, we get the extra pay to cover their collective asses. As far as contact and the B.C.U protocols, they are overridden, as contact has already been established."

Trofim had known there was more than what he had been told, and even now he doubted that Millerton had told him everything, but that was the way the game was played. Sometimes it was best not to know everything, unless that information could keep you from getting killed. However, the money was nice…or it was going to be when he got home. That was the only upside to taking an American contract—they paid well. And as soon as he got out of this place, he was leaving the killing and all of this black ops sneaky crap to the others.

"Some of this would have been good to know a little earlier." Tro stared at the ground and thought of the Chinstrap. If the thing could actually speak, and not just say words like a parrot, then it could have been interrogated. "I still think you shouldn't have killed that penguin," he said, slinging his automatic weapon.

"After what has happened, all penguins are considered hostile to our employers. And yes, some of it would have helpful to know, but just know I'm breaking my end of *my* contract to tell you these things," Millerton said. He leaned in close and looked at Trofim pointedly. "I don't trust Jenson and neither should you. He has his own motives, and I have no clue what they are. And honestly, you're the only person I trust."

Trofim looked out at Forward Command looming in the distance. He couldn't shake the feeling that something life changing was going to happen today, and hopefully it wouldn't be life ending. He looked back at Millerton with a certain sadness. "Well, I can't say that I trust you, Zach."

Millerton nodded. "I can't say that I blame you."

The two men went to their respective vehicles. Trofim climbed in and took a seat drawing a look from Alyssa. "What was all of that about?"

Tro kept his eyes forward. "Just talking baseball."

CHAPTER 8

General Talus pulled his head back from a narrow slit in the front wall of the outpost. "Did you see that?" he said with twisted glee. "These Kaurochs are just what we've needed. How the Overlord and his bloated buffoon of a *Supreme Commander* couldn't see the usefulness of our brothers is beyond me."

Cryzyrky did her best to shrug. Standing only two foot tall, there was no way she could see through the narrow openings, which resembled the arrow slits that adorned the walls of ancient fortresses, and instead relied on Talus' enthusiastic descriptions. His enthusiasm was contagious. Cryzyrky, along with others, felt energized and eager to meet their enemy. A Kauroch surfaced through the enlarged hole at the center of the compound, and Talus was quick to meet his new favorite weapon.

After listening to a series of barely audible grunts, Talus instructed the behemoth to move on to the next phase. He met the eyes of a Royal Emperor after the Kauroch departed. "Get the long pikes ready. The humans are falling directly into our trap," he crowed. The penguins who had been under his command during previous skirmishes were used to the Warlord's excitement when the time came to kill. Talus suspected that Antaean had an ulterior motive to sending out the bulk of the Penguin Defense Alliance to face the enemy on its terms, but the Overlord always had ulterior motives and schemes, and the Warlord always kept that in mind.

Talus regarded the Kaurochs once again. They added the missing element which he felt would ensure victory. If they could deprive the humans of their machinery, they would be as helpless as an abandoned seal pup. His original plan had been to meet them with brute force at Forward Command, then withdraw further inland behind the rifts where they could only follow on foot. The Kaurochs made him revise his plan, and it had begun exactly as he had envisioned.

Cryzyrky approached Talus. She wanted to have a word in private, and judging by the look in his eyes, she had limited time before he was consumed by battle frenzy. "Talus, I'm having second thoughts about this plan. I think moving inland would serve us best."

Talus considered her words, and for a moment, he seemed to mull it over. "Cryzyrky, I understand your apprehension. And I assure you, if this goes poorly, we will make our escape. But this is our defining moment. All that we have fought through before, throughout all of the incursions and raids, we have never been tested. The humans have come here with the intent to kill us all. Not just us here, but all penguins. If we cannot survive this encounter, then how will we fare once the Overlord is defeated? And trust me, he will be defeated; it is only a matter of time. We will take what we learn today and use it to our advantage. It is key to our survival."

"And if we don't survive today?"

"If we cannot survive today, then what makes you think tomorrow will be any different?"

Cryzryky looked away. She wondered what made him think that this was his defining moment. She had heard him speak of a visit to a so-called Oracle, and it was she who told him of his destiny. Cryzryky thought his belief in the Ancients was the Warlord's only weakness. Invisible spirits of long dead penguins controlling destinies and mad penguins claiming they could speak with them was more than she could accept. The living controlled their own fate—sure, coincidences occurred which made it appear as if the lives of common penguins were guided along certain paths, but she refused to put her faith in coincidence. Oracles and Ancient gods be damned, she had no choice but to put her faith in the Warlord. She was about to comment on his faith when it hit her—who among the living did Talus have to look to for guidance and protection? Talus was the apex of the penguin warrior culture. Unburdened by the desire for empires or rule, unencumbered by law, he was alone.

In that instant, she discovered a new respect for Talus in knowing he didn't see himself as the ascendant of all things. She looked at Talus, who stood proud and tall, in the face of what could very well be his last day on this world.

"May the Spirits of the Ancients be at our side," she said. Her eyes smiled as she walked away.

Talus watched her go. "Now there is a penguin I would lay down my life for," he said quietly. A Chinstrap penguin messenger popped out of the seal hole, pulling him from his reverie.

"Sir," the Chinstrap said. "Supreme Commander Liutites demands an update."

Talus laughed aloud. "Tell that bloated seal carcass to come to the front and see for himself, if he has the courage," he said.

The Chinstrap was uncertain what to do next. "Sir," the messenger nervously stammered. "If you don't mind, if I deliver that message, it will likely lead to my death."

Talus loomed large over the Chinstrap and laughed. "Indeed it would. Tell him that the battle has begun and he will receive an update once it is over," Talus said, much to the relief of the Chinstrap.

"Sir," a Royal said when the messenger departed. "The humans are on the move."

"Excellent. See to it that the long pikes are ready. They will have no choice but scale the ramparts." The fire had returned to his eyes in a flash. He gripped his own pike tightly in anticipation of the kill. "Let them come to us."

CHAPTER 9

The crawlers' speed matched their name. They couldn't move faster than the men walking ahead, who were searching for more pitfalls. Trofim's crew took the lead. The passengers sat in tense silence, hoping they wouldn't hear the crack of ice. One of the scouts flagged Fob, and he brought the crawler to a stop. Trofim threw open the door. "What is it?" he asked impatiently. The idea of stopping and letting the weight of the vehicle rest on the ice made him extremely nervous.

"We spotted a total of six other dig outs, on either side of our current path," the man said, panting.

"On either side?" Tro asked, not liking where this was going. "How wide is our avenue?"

"Approximately twenty-five meters," the other answered, scanning the surroundings for danger.

"They definitely want us to go this way. I don't think we have a choice."

Padre spoke up from the rear seat. "We *do* have a choice. We could just get out here, walk in, and send them all to face judgment."

"Lieutenant Millerton's orders are to drive close. I'm not sure why, but I'm assuming it has something to do with setting up another operations base," Tro said. He raised a hand to cut off further protest. "Okay, tell the others to get back to their vehicles. Millerton, are you hearing this?"

"Yep," the lieutenant said through the headset.

"We are going in hard and fast from this point on. I have the feeling there are some more surprises awaiting at the end. I suggest we stop fifty meters in front of the target. That should give us enough time to react to anything they have planned. Boots on the ground, running," Tro said. He checked to make sure the others had gotten back to their crawler. "Let's do this things."

Even with the stress of impending combat looming, A-Bomb had to laugh at Trofim's wording. She had to wonder if he did it sometimes just to ease the tension. Even if it wasn't intentional, it worked. She stared through the passenger window, each foggy breath quickly wiped away by the relatively warm air of the defroster. She took a deep, cleansing breath and let it out nice and slow, mimicking Trofim's meditations. She closed her eyes to reach a focused calm.

Screams of warning shocked Alyssa out of her meditation. She opened her eyes and spotted a huge black object sliding across the ice, directly at their vehicle. Clawed, gull wings pulled the creature closer, and it looked as if it were going to slam into her door. She felt Trofim's powerful arms pull her away from the impending impact. They braced for the strike, but it didn't come right away. The Kauroch had reared up on its small back legs, extending itself to its full height of ten feet, and fell with all of its massive weight against the vehicle.

The last-minute lurch brought the Kauroch's impact toward the rear of the crawler. It hit the rear passenger window with such strength that that the beast's clawed arm shattered the tempered glass. The sheer brute force of the collision caused the vehicle to spin to its right. The Kauroch clung to the vehicle, blindly groping the interior to find purchase.

Dik-dik struggled to remove his seatbelt as he tried to dodge the four-inch claws. He didn't dare take his eyes off of the probing arm, for fear that it would tear into him. He felt the release, but the clawed arm swung at him. He leaned out of the way. The Kauroch tore through the seat where his shoulder had been a fraction of a second before. Dik-dik felt for the release, letting out a triumphant swear when he finally freed himself from the bondage. He leaned across Padre's lap, trying to avoid another swipe.

Padre pulled Dik-dik toward him when the Kauroch reached again. The beast's claws snagged Dik-dik's coat and pulled him toward the window. Padre and Parker screamed, locked in a vicious tug-of-war over their comrade. Dik-dik felt fabric rip away and he let out a sigh, happy to be free once again. Within a heartbeat, his relief turned to horror. Kauroch's claw found his throat. There was barely time for him to let out a gargled cry before his trachea was torn in half. Blood sprayed across the cabin when the claws ripped through his carotid artery. The Kauroch lost its hold for good.

Once the weight of Kauroch was off of the crawler, the vehicle came to a rest. Trofim and Alyssa immediately looked back. Dik-dik was already unconscious; he would be dead within a minute. The entirety of the attack had taken less than thirty seconds. Trofim and A-Bomb sprang from the crawler, just in time to see another attack.

The crawler behind Trofim's had stopped. The second Kauroch rammed the vehicle hard on the driver's side. The bird's large spade beak broke through the window, killing the driver instantly. The Kauroch that had attacked Trofim's crawler quickly slid across the ice, toward the vehicle, as the other beast shattered more glass with its massive beak. The surviving passengers tried to flee through the other side. With a mighty groan of metal, the combined weight and strength of the two Kaurochs flipped the crawler on its side, crushing the escapees.

Trofim got his weapon in firing position. One burst was all he needed to make the first Kauroch's head explode. He took vicious satisfaction as the beast slumped to the ground without as much as a twitch. He shifted his aim to where the second monster had been, but it was already sliding across the ice toward its escape. He was surprised by its speed. He tried to get a bead on the fleeing creature, but the overturned crawler lay between it and Trofim. Instead of giving chase, Tro ran to assist the others.

When he arrived, Trofim saw there wasn't anything that could be done.

Two of the men had been crushed by the weight of the vehicle. Millerton was shouting out orders to hook up a winch to try to pull the crawler upright. People were screaming profanities. Some pled for help.

"The winch will just drag the crawler. It will have to be lifted. We don't have time for that," Tro said. He didn't like the idea of leaving the dead men where they were, but they had little choice.

Millerton reluctantly agreed. He turned to tell Trofim what to do next, but he was already on the other side of the crawler, inspecting the dead Kauroch. "Have you ever seen anything like this?"

Trofim looked at the lieutenant incredulously. When would have he ever encountered an oversized mutated penguin? He turned his attention back to the corpse. "I was about to ask you the same question. This wasn't on the list," he answered.

"Nobody told me. This is a pretty big oversight if anyone knew about them," he said, watching Trofim pace the length of the dead animal.

"Three or four meters. A very big oversight," Tro said. He surveyed their surroundings. "We should go in on foot. These things aren't immune to bullets."

They jerked, hearing a loud pop near one of the other crawlers. Trofim's eyes widened. "Get that crawler moving," he yelled.

"On it," Fob yelled back, sprinting toward the crawler. He reached for the door. The ice started to give way, and Fob yanked his hand back. He jumped backwards and landed awkwardly. From his prone position, he saw the vehicle lurch sideways. The ground began to angle downward and he tried to crab-walk, digging his spiked boots into the frozen ground. Spinning and flailing, desperately trying to get to his feet, the ice gave. His eyes widened, knowing he was headed to a freezing death. He felt a tug on his shoulder, then another. Padre and A-Bomb yanked him to his feet. The trio ran to safety as the crawler sank into the sea.

Trofim and Millerton looked on in disbelief. They were stuck. If they left the crawlers behind, the ice would be dug out beneath them; if they drove, they took the chance of driving into more traps. "On foot or drive?" Tro asked.

"*You* can drive," Fob told Trofim. "I'm going in on foot. I'm going to march up there and blow their waddling asses back to hell." He patted the forend of his shotgun.

Trofim looked at Millerton. "You call Jenson or whoever the hell is in charge and tell them the situation. We're moving out…now." Already down nine men in less than ten minutes, he wasn't taking any more chances.

Millerton hesitated as if he were about to argue, but nodded instead. "Grab all of the weapons you can carry. Like you said, we go in quick and hard. I'll be right behind you." Without another word, he trotted to his crawler to call for back-up and possible extraction.

Within minutes, the remaining soldiers had gathered their weapons and grouped around Trofim. "Watch your backs, stay alert, and watch your cross-fire. Let's move," Trofim said. They began moving at steady but slow run toward Forward Command.

CHAPTER 10

"A trench? Are you kidding me?" A-Bomb said. "What are we dealing with here? They said these things were smart, but come on."

"Well at least we know the ice is thicker here. No chance of us falling in," Padre said.

A-Bomb gave him a wry look. "Some consolation. Do we know what's on the other side?" she turned to Trofim.

"We'll know when we get there," Tro said. He cautiously stepped into the trench and studied the battlements. Seams in the ice ran up and across the surface, and narrow gaps gave the bulwark the appearance of a haphazardly constructed igloo. The face stood two meters tall from base to top, but the trench added another two feet of height. He hopped back across the furrow and looked down the length of the fortification. "I don't see any other way around. Who wants to go up for a look?"

No hands were raised, and no one stepped forward. "Parker, you're up," Tro said to the tallest of the group.

Parker shook his head. "I hate being the tall one."

"Just a quick peek, and let us know what you see."

"I can see through this crack," Parker said, pointing to the slit in the wall. He stood on his toes on the narrow precipice between the trench and the wall, pressing his face against the façade. "I can see light. Walls appear to be about four-feet thick."

"Anything else?" Padre asked. "Any signs of movement?"

"I can't tell. There's something in the way. Looks like …" He squinted, looking for anything else, and was about to give up when a shadow blocked out the light. "Wait. I see move—"

It took a half a second for him to realize that he was looking a penguin in the eye on the opposite end of the wall. The end of the sharpened pike stabbed him through his eye with enough force to break the sphenoid bone at the back of his eye socket. He let out a brief yell, flew backwards, and landed unconscious in the gully.

Multiple shouts rang out. Padre grabbed the limp body and dragged him out of the trench. A-Bomb took her gun, put the barrel in the slit, and squeezed off a couple bursts.

"Hold your fire," Trofim yelled. "Save your ammo for targets. Tinker, what does it look like?" he asked the young man, who was both a medic and demolitions expert.

Tinker knelt over Parker, looking at the wound and feeling for a pulse. He looked back at Trofim and shook his head. "Not good, Sarge. Pulse is weak."

Trofim swore and opened his mic to the lieutenant. "Millerton, get that crawler up here now. Man down. We need immediate Evac."

"Making the call, and I'm on my way," Millerton's voice squelched through the ear piece.

"Are you sure that's a good idea?" Fob asked, wary of the lieutenant driving the oversized vehicle.

"We don't have any options. It's his only hope," Trofim said. He knew it was a huge risk, but they really didn't have any other choice. If they could get Parker in the vehicle and stabilize him with the limited medical supplies they had, he stood a chance, albeit a small one. He stood rigid, biting the inside of his cheek, watching the command vehicle begin its slow drive forward. He turned to face the others. "Here's the plan. After we get Parker in the vehicle, we line the wall. Grenades go over, then we follow."

"Sounds good, boss," A-Bomb said. She watched Tinker hold the back of Parker's head. Parker's body quaked, then went lax. She watched as Tinker felt for a pulse. His eyes met hers, and she knew any evac would just be to retrieve the body. She walked back to Trofim, who had turned his attention back to Millerton's progress. "Tro…"

Tro turned, and when their eyes met he saw the eternal glint of cheer absent. His eyes fell on Tinker, who stood and un-shouldered his weapon. Parker was dead. Trofim let out a sigh and glanced at A-Bomb. She fixed him with a strangely mischievous stare, her eyebrow raised. Her lively expression returned almost as quickly as it had left. She had that look that Trofim had grown to know. The look that said something was about to die, and it was going to die violently.

Her look rejuvenated Trofim. She always seemed to have that effect on him. His eyes narrowed as he gave her a half grin and he turned to check on Millerton's progress. He turned and saw the front of the lieutenant's vehicle rise in the air as the back end fell through the ice. For a man who prided himself in the fact that he rarely swore, today was not a day to be proud of.

He began to run toward the crawler, even knowing there wasn't a damn thing he could do. The freezing water would devour Millerton, the same as it had the others.

Before the water swallowed the vehicle completely, Trofim spotted the lieutenant picking himself up off of the ice. The crawler disappeared below the surface while Millerton, cursing, stood at a safe distance from the hole. The lieutenant looked toward Sergeant Grekov and walked dejectedly toward him. Just then, Tro spotted something springing from the breach. Not something, but several somethings. A half a dozen penguins were coming up behind the lieutenant, who seemed to be unaware of the danger.

"Behind you," Tro shouted.

Millerton turned around just before the first assailant had reached him. They were smaller, regular sized penguins; three Rockhoppers, two

Gentoo, and an Adélie. A Rockhopper led the group. Millerton kicked the creature with such force that he had to stare in admiration of the distance a well-punted penguin could fly. He turned to run, fishing his side-arm out as he did. Antarctica may be the domain of the penguins, but even a penguin couldn't move with speed on the ice. Millerton, with his spiked boots had no such problem. After putting some distance between him and his pursuers, he turned and fired five consecutive shots, each bullet finding its target. He brought his aim on the punted penguin, but it slipped back into the hole before he could fire.

"Nice shooting," Trofim said with a smirk. "Five shots, five kills."

Millerton shook his head. "I have to conserve. I only have three magazines, and my M4 is at the bottom of the sea," he said, cussing. "Who's down?"

"Parker," Tro said, shaking his head. "It's too late. We lost your crawler for naught. Did you make the call at least?"

"Our only ride out will be if someone comes to get us."

"No support then?"

Millerton shook his head. "No back up anyways, I don't know about anything else. They weren't clear about that. Do we know what's on the other side of that wall yet?" he asked as they walked.

"Something with sharp sticks."

"They're armed? Well shit on me. Just shit on me and get it over with. How the hell does a penguin know how to use a weapon? Or better yet, how can it even *hold* a weapon? And while we're at it, how the hell do they know how to speak English and build crap and…ah, forget it."

Trofim let the man vent. When Millerton was done, Tro just shrugged. He surveyed Forward Command once more, trying to see another way in other than surmounting the wall. The jagged ice on either end of the walls would be difficult to climb, and it would take time they didn't have. They had wasted too much daylight already. He explained his plan of leading with a grenade barrage. "This is like fighting primitives. Their weapons are crude, but their tactics are sound. They've outwitted us on every move since we got here. They've been waiting for us."

"No doubt," Millerton agreed. "Well at least they don't have guns—"

"That we know of," Tro interjected.

"Be that as it may, we'll go on what we do know. And from the looks of it, it seems that they have limited numbers. If there were thousands of them, they would have just come at us from behind, en masse, instead of sending a handful of sacrifices. They would've had us pinned against the wall and we wouldn't have been able to hold out—especially if they had more of those big sons-of-bitches. No, they're limited. Maybe two hundred of them…if that," Millerton concluded when they reached the others.

A thunderous crash from behind them made both men spin, weapons ready. They turned in time to see the last crawler fall beneath the ice. The two men cursed in unison.

"Let's hope they actually do send a chopper," Tro said. "Alright, people, you know the plan. Let's get to it. They know we're here and they're waiting. Let's give them what they want."

CHAPTER 11

The Kauroch breeched the surface and slid beside General Talus, who was waiting with the patience and glee of a man who had taught his dog to fetch. While he was disappointed by the death of the second Kauroch, he was more than satisfied at what the one remaining creature had accomplished. All of the human machines now lay on the seafloor. It was unfortunate that his third Kauroch had to remain out of the impending fray, but a chariot for him to live and fight another day was a necessity in this situation, and only because of Cryzryky. She would have to be the one to deliver the news to the Overlord if the Ancients decided that today was the day he was to meet his fate. But Talus, knowing the Overlord's volatility when receiving bad news, vowed to himself that he would not allow her to die for his loss. Even the idea of the waiting Kauroch showed that Talus was, for the first time in his long history of combat, not certain of the outcome. The small victories already obtained were but trivial to the Warlord; he knew the real fight was yet to come.

"Sir," a Royal Emperor said. "They are preparing to surmount the wall."

"Details, Metholeces. What did they say?"

"They are against the outer wall and will lead with grenades. I'm sorry, sir, but I do not know what grenades means."

Talus pondered the information. Whatever a grenade was or is, he knew it would not be pleasant. "To the top of the parapet. Push the blocks on their heads and let us find out."

The most able-bodied Royal Emperors, former elite warriors of the Overlord, climbed the narrow ramp to the top of the rampart. Several loose blocks of ice lay waiting for just such an eventuality. The penguins placed the tops of their heads against the first block, dug into the ice with their powerful legs, and began to shove. They could hear the voice of a man on the other side of the wall begin to count down, and by the time the man reached one, the block fell over the side.

Several people shouted below the wall, and the penguins peered over to see their work. They spotted a human lying on the ground, twitching in his death throes, with the nearly one hundred pound broken block of ice resting where his head had been. For a brief moment, they were confused at seeing the other humans running from where the dead man lay. A second later, they found out why, when the grenade he had been holding detonated. The two Royal Emperors flew off the wall, knocking a third down with them as they fell.

Talus saw the bloodied faces of the penguins and knew immediately what grenades were. "Back! All of you to the rear wall. Now!" Seconds later, he turned to see several grenades flying over the barricade. He instinctively ducked and turned his body away as multiple explosions went off. He felt tiny bits of ice and other debris rain down on his body; some stinging, others bouncing harmlessly off of his seal leather tunic.

When the icy dust settled, Talus surveyed the damage. At least ten penguins who hadn't cleared the fifteen meter blast radius were dead or dying. He felt his body quake with rage and he gripped his pike. "To the top of the walls. They're coming over," he barked. The battle had begun, and now it was his turn to spill his enemy's blood.

At hearing the Warlord's orders, twenty Royal Emperors ran to ramps at either end of the wall. The remaining penguins, consisting of Adélie, Gentoo, Rockhopper, Kings, and Chinstraps dove into the hole to await their turn. Talus followed Cryzyrky into the alcove at the rear of the command post. "If I should fall here, get to the Kauroch. Do not go to Pack Ice Command. Seek out the Alliance. They will take you in," he told her.

"If you die here, then so will I," Cryzyrky said.

"No," Talus said with a tone that left no room for argument. "You have to live. You must tell their leader, the Chinstrap called Lavour, or the Gentoo called Leepoh, about the Basileios. I doubt they know the significance or that they even exist. They are the true threat. If they resurface in full, then they can wipe out the Royals and subjugate all of the clans, like they did after the Auk War. Overlord Antaean knows this. That is why he imprisoned Saeson, and that is why he seeks out Aperion. No more protests. Our future depends on it, unless the humans kill us all first."

Cryzryky wanted to object further, but now was not the time. If what he was saying was true, then this war was just the beginning. The thought of being left alone without Talus was a thought she refused to entertain. He would live. He had to live. If he didn't, then she would honor his request, but nothing more, and hope that he was right in his faith. Then they would meet again in the Great Sea.

The first human pulled himself up to the top of the wall, unslinging and shucking his shotgun in one motion. He trained the gun to the right on his nearest opponent, who was charging in with pike forward. The blast sent the penguin flying back into his comrades, toppling them over. He shucked the gun once more, but the Royal charging from the man's left drove its spear tip through the meat of the man's thigh. The man screamed and fell to one knee. The penguin withdrew the spear and drove it through the man's throat, ending the threat.

A second and third human appeared on the wall. The first of them fell immediately by a spear tip through the gut, but the other managed to bring his weapon to firing position and rain hell on the penguins, who had pushed their fallen comrades' bodies aside and continued the charge. A fourth person lifted his head over the precipice, only to have it pierced through the mouth and out the back of his skull. The human firing the weapon spun and laid waste to the other's killer.

Several more humans climbed the wall and brought their weapons to bear on the penguins. Pin feathers and blood flew through the air as one penguin after another was cut down. A human on the far end of the wall became overzealous in his killing, and paid the price of a spear tip thrust through his back. His attacker withdrew the spear and finished the job by driving the spear through the base of the man's skull. With no more targets, the human soldiers began helping their compatriots up on to the wall. They kicked the bodies of the penguins aside and began making a cautious descent off the parapet.

Talus peered out from the alcove, watching the human's progress. Although disturbed by how quickly they had killed twenty elite warriors, he knew this fight was not over yet. "Good," he said quietly. "Come closer, just like a good warrior should."

CHAPTER 12

"Watch yourselves, there may be more," Sergeant Grekov said, watching what was left of the squads descend into the courtyard of Forward Command. After helping Lieutenant Millerton to the top of the wall with a great tug of his arm, Trofim surveyed the interior of the command post. The acrid stench of guano stung his nose. He noticed that the mess was deposited in one corner of the outpost, much like a latrine. He tried to gauge just how many penguins were had been there based on the amount of waste. It seemed like a lot.

Looking toward the back wall, nearly fifty meters from where he stood, Trofim spotted an alcove and another opening. Not an arched entryway like the alcove, but just a gap in the wall. Obviously, whoever had constructed the fortification wasn't concerned about an attack from the interior, only an assault from the coastal areas. They were protecting something inland. He scanned the horizon behind Forward Command. The blue sky touched faint purple mountains, which loomed behind enormous formations of azure blue and turquoise ice, like splashes of color on a blank canvas. He could have stood and marveled at the beauty of it all for an hour, had he not spotted a solitary black figure resting against the brilliant white back drop. "Give me your glasses," Tro said to Millerton.

Millerton looked at Trofim with a bit of confusion and started to pull off his orange-tinted UV goggles. Trofim slapped him in the stomach. "No. The…the binoculars," he said, putting too much emphasis on the U.

Millerton handed them over, and asked what he was looking at, which Trofim didn't answer. Tro got a better look at the figure—another Kauroch. He scanned the landscape for more, but spotted none. He found the Kauroch once more and noticed the sled attached to the creature. He handed the binoculars back to the lieutenant, who asked again. Tro simply pointed to the black spot on the white ice. Tro rested his weapon against his shoulder and put the creature in the sights. He felt wind blowing from the east against his face, and adjusted his aim slightly to left and up. He considered the wind and maximum effective range of his M4 and lowered the weapon. If he shot and missed, he would simply spook the animal and that would serve no real purpose. And with most of their supplies lying on the seabed, ammunition was best conserved.

"Sergeant Grekov, you better have a look at this," Tinker said.

Trofim and Millerton hopped off the wall to where Tinker was kneeling down, holding a dead Royal Emperor's head up. "Notice anything unusual about their beaks?"

Trofim leaned in and rubbed his hand along a metallic tip on the beak. The metallic addition took up an inch of the dead Royal's five inch long beak. Trofim wriggled and pried, trying to loosen the deadly-looking beak enhancement. "That's a snug fit," he said, finally popping it free.

Millerton examined the steel beak. "I wonder how they made these?" He looked at Trofim, eyes wide, realizing just how complicit GT was in this war. Tro just shook his head.

"Okay, I can see maybe, and I do mean *maybe*, fashioning spears out of teeth and bone. And being as how they seem to have developed articulated hands, maybe even building a fortress," A-Bomb said, waving her hands at the command post. "Lord knows I've seen stranger things. But how the hell can a penguin forge metal? Are you telling me they have a foundry buried somewhere beneath the ice and they manufacture these things?

Never mind the impossibility of finding fuel here to run the furnace, or the tell-tale sign of the necessary smokestacks. No, there's no way. This is bullshit. Somebody's helping them."

When A-Bomb finished her rant, all eyes were on Lieutenant Millerton. "How the hell should I know?" he lied, throwing his arms in the air in exasperation.

"Jenson didn't mention the beaks to you?" Trofim asked, looking more than a little upset.

"No…nothing. Believe me, after we mop this mess up, I'm going to have more than a few questions for him," Millerton said. He was tired of defending himself to Trofim. True, there were things that Trofim didn't need to know, but obviously there were things that Colonel Jenson felt that the lieutenant didn't need to know. "And speaking of which—spread out. Let's finish this up and see if there is anything of value we can find here. And watch that hole. We don't one of those big sonsabitches to pop up and drag one of us down with it." Those closest to the enlarged seal-hole looked at it and took several steps away.

When the others spread out, Trofim put his arm around Alyssa. "You hit the head of the nail with your hammer," he said quietly. "We'll talk after we're done."

"About?" Alyssa asked, her eyes meeting his with a mischievous glint.

Trofim opened his mouth, but no words were forthcoming. His eyes locked on hers, and for a moment he thought of the future, a future where he wasn't alone. "About a few things," he finally stammered. She smiled.

The wind swirled inside the compound, picking the loose pin-feathers of the dead penguins, making them dance through the air. The silence and utter lack of movement otherwise created a palpable tension amongst the soldiers. They walked in two meter spreads in total silence, waiting to hear a revelatory sound that something was alive and watching them.

A noise finally made itself known. A tiny, barely audible warble, coming from the most logical and predictable place: the alcove.

Guns trained on the four foot tall opening, waiting for something to spring forward. Eager fingers resisted the urge to pull the triggers when sound came again. Trofim made a gesture and Fob inched closer. The crunch of spiked boots seemed to overpower the steady whistle of the wind. So focused on their target, no one heard the first splash of a wet body landing on the ice. Only movement in the peripheral of her sight made A-Bomb turn and look. "Behind us," she shouted.

Where there was one penguin, soon there were five, followed by ten more, followed by another dozen. Those penguins that hadn't been dispatched immediately closed the gap quickly and attempted to drive their sharp beaks through the layers of clothing on the soldier's legs. One man fired as a beak found its mark on the back of his leg, and he raked gunfire through the body of another man.

"Goddamnit, watch your crossfire," Millerton shouted, seeing another man go down to friendly fire.

The squaddie who had accidentally killed his comrade lifted his spiked boot high and brought it down hard on his assailant's head. He ran to check on the man he accidentally shot, but another twenty penguins leapt from the sea, tripping him. He fell hard and the penguins took advantage. They savagely pecked any exposed areas with the precision of combat experience. The man called for help, but everyone else was busy with their own entanglements. His attackers suddenly dispersed to other frays before they finished their job. Confused by their quick departure, he took a second to regain his wits. The injuries were painful, but not life threatening. He began to sit up just as the Kauroch made its appearance. It fell on the man with its full weight, driving its spade beak through his chest, and dragged its victim into the water.

Trofim, knife in hand, had just lopped off the head of a Chinstrap when he saw the Kauroch appear. He had seen what it was about to do, but Tro could do nothing to prevent it. He called to Millerton, closest to the Kauroch, but he had his hands full dealing with three Rockhoppers who were deftly evading his kicks and strikes. Trofim saw the Kauroch disappear, and gave up on any heroics. Finding a break in assailants, he sheathed his knife and drew his Colt. He took careful aim and neatly plucked two of Millerton's attackers. The lieutenant took advantage of the break and stomped at the third Rockhopper, who fled. Trofim fired another perfect shot, dropping the penguin as it ran.

However, Trofim's and Millerton's break was fleeting. Another two-dozen penguins shot from the water. They joined in the fray as fast as their wet feet hit the ice. Trofim took aim, but there wasn't a clear shot. The other soldiers were all engaged in hand combat. He looked at Millerton, who returned his gaze. Both men drew their blades and stepped into the fracas.

CHAPTER 13

Talus peered out of the alcove and watched with satisfaction at the melee taking place. Penguins were dying with great expediency, which upset the Warlord. It was unfortunate, but necessary, and there was no other way around it. His plan was coming to fruition. Two humans had already been killed within the confines of the outpost, and several more were about to be. He called out a warble similar to the one he had used to lure the humans to one side of the redoubt. The humans couldn't hear it this time; the cacophony of squawking birds and shouting men drowned out the noise to all but the discerning ear.

Across the enclosure, three Royal Emperors thought killed by the humans stirred from beneath the bodies of their fallen comrades. Each gripped their spears and replied with a series of guttural clicks. Slowly they began to move forward, lying on their stomachs, propelling themselves with clawed feet. Their belly-sliding was slow and thoughtful, no sudden movements to draw attention—just a dark mass that moved a foot every half a minute.

Talus watched the Royal's progress. He gripped his pike tightly in anticipation of making his first kill. He forced himself to stay where he was, but the draw of battle was tugging at him. The lure of bloodshed was a physical thing, gripping his body and pulling him ever closer to the midst of the fray. He clenched his beak and resisted the urge. When the Royals reached their first target, the one the others called Lieutenant, he would make his move then. It was a patience he was not used to exercising. And when a human stumbled backward and nearly fell into the alcove, the urge became too much to resist.

Talus sprung from the opening and met the eyes of the surprised human, who wore hair which draped down longer than the Warlord's own yellow head plumage. Before the human could react, Talus drove his pike under the man's chin, puncturing the soft flesh. The man's white teeth bared, in either impotent rage or grimacing pain of death, Talus didn't care. It was his first kill in many days, and he delighted in seeing the man crumple to the ground when he withdrew the spear.

Shouts of alarmed humans rang out; calls of *Fob* echoed. What a fob was, Talus didn't know. Perhaps it was his first victim's name, but it mattered little. He was now in full bloodlust. The human nearest him drew its gun. Talus swung his pike down and struck the barrel away before the bullets found their mark. Instead, the gun fired uselessly into the ice. He raised his pike up and thrust it in the face of his would-be attacker. It wasn't a killing blow, but it was enough to blind his attacker in one eye. The human screamed in agony and Talus gave him the mercy of a quick death as he drove the elongated spear through its rib-cage and heart.

The Warlord saw his next quarry. It was almost too easy—the man had his back turned to him, and had he cared, he would have felt guilty for driving his weapon through the man's back. Three kills in less than a minute. These humans were supposed to be fierce, he thought. He marched toward his next target, who had been preoccupied with a menagerie of smaller penguins attacking him. Talus brought his pike to bear, but as he thrust forward, the human spun and took hold of his pike, wresting it from his grip.

The man let out a laugh. "Not so tough now, are you?" the man taunted.

Talus' eyes narrowed. "As a matter of fact I am," he said in perfect English. The man's eyes widened in surprise at hearing him speak. Talus jabbed his beak into his chest. He felt the flutter of the man's heart against his beak as it made its final beat.

He pulled his beak from the man's chest, retrieved his pike, and spotted the Royal assassins as they were about to make their move. His look of satisfaction was short-lived when a well planted kick knocked him to the ground. He lost his grip on his pike and fell face first, sliding to a stop against the back wall of the fortification.

Several Rockhoppers attacked the man who had kicked him, giving Talus a chance for recovery. "The Ancients are with me on this day," he said. He looked for his pike and spotted it lying amongst seven penguins and one man engaged in combat. He felt for the gift Cryzyrky had given him, and giving silent thanks, pulled the weapon from its holster. His attacker had just thrown the last of his assailants aside and looked at Talus in time to see the squared club swinging at him. All the man could do was flinch as the club found the side of his head.

Talus watched in satisfaction as the man fell, unconscious before he hit the ground. He beat the man's skull twice more, feeling the sickly crunch of cranial bone on the second strike. He struck a third time just for pleasure. Talus let out an unearthly roar in triumph as several more penguins flew from the depths to assist in the battle. The day would be his. The Ancients were at his side and he could feel their power flowing through him. He gripped his new favored weapon tightly and moved to the next kill.

CHAPTER 14

Trofim fought with his eight-inch blade in one hand and his Colt in the other. His M4 hung uselessly on his back, unable to be used in these close quarters. He watched helplessly from the corner of his eye as the large newcomer bashed Tinker's skull. This was a creature of a different ilk, and it had to be dealt with quickly. He separated a Rockhopper's head from its body and fired two successive shots from his .45, killing two more. He pulled the trigger to finish off another, but his magazine was empty. A Rockhopper leaped toward him, and Trofim met it with his knife through its body. He let the weight of the penguin's seven pound body rest on the blade while he sliced upward, nearly bisecting the creature. He flung the dead bird from his blade and stepped on it for good measure. It was unlike him to expend the extra energy of double-tapping an already dead opponent during a fight, but he was starting to get annoyed by these things.

He holstered his empty side-arm and moved toward the newcomer, who had killed four fully trained soldiers in less than two minutes time. Fob was dead; Tinker was dead, and a few others who he had barely known were dead. He checked A-Bomb, who was gleefully kicking, stomping and stabbing her opponents with a somewhat disturbing mirth. Padre was holding his own, but Trofim noticed dark blood stains on his pant legs where beaks had found their mark. He looked to Millerton, who was having a time with his own half dozen attackers.

Tro had stooped down to neatly decapitate another bird when he spotted movement behind the lieutenant. Two Royal Emperors stood up and raised their spears. Tro shouted a warning and started to run to the lieutenant's aid. He sheathed his knife and pulled his M4 from his shoulder, no longer giving a damn about cross fire. He didn't see the Kauroch lunge from the water. The beast hit Trofim with such force that it lifted him from his feet, sending him flailing five feet through the air. His weapon flew twice that distance and slid another ten feet out of reach. His head slammed hard against the ice, and it was all he could do to keep from blacking out. Instinct took over and he tried to shake the stars from his head as he stood. His legs fell out from under him. Resting on hands and knees, he braced for the inevitable follow up attack. Trofim's senses returned—he wasn't going to die this easily. He grabbed his knife and spun his body around, with blade in the lead, hoping to slash the creature's throat. His blade met nothing but air. Surprised but relieved, he got to his feet in time to see the Kauroch disappear back through the hole, with another victim in its beak. As lucky as Trofim had been, Millerton was not.

Zach Millerton spun to face his attackers, only to feel two spears lance his midsection. He screamed through the burning pain, bringing his pistol up. He pointed it in the face of one of his killers and pulled the trigger, getting the satisfaction of seeing the birds head splatter the other with blood and brain matter before he fell. The smaller penguins descended on the lieutenant to finish the job.

Trofim fought off several Adélie, making quick work of them, and moved toward the leather clad penguin who had just brained another soldier. He was dimly aware of A-Bomb screaming a battle cry while emptying her M4 into Millerton's killers. The gunfire reverberated off of the ice walls, mixing with the bleats of dying and murderous penguins to create a chaotic din. When A-Bomb's magazine was emptied, the relative silence revealed the moans of dying men and penguin alike.

"A-Bomb," Trofim shouted. When she didn't respond, he called again. "Alyssa, pick your targets. Take care of the big one."

As if responding to the command to kill its master, the Kauroch reappeared. The behemoth sprung from the ice-hole and reared up to its full height, intending to fall on A-Bomb. Alyssa was fishing out another magazine when she heard Padre shout her name. She looked up to see the massive shadow of a beast looming over her. "Oh crap," she said, just before Padre knocked her out of the way.

The Kauroch fell on Alyssa's savior, pinning him to the ice. Padre's eyes bulged under the weight of the monster. A stabbing pain in his sides told him that one or more ribs had been broken He reached for A-Bomb with a pleading hand. A-Bomb had been knocked to the ground by Padre's shove and was attempting to stand when a Gentoo hopped her back and pecked at her nape. She swore, twisted her body, and grabbed the twelve pound Gentoo by the neck. She stood, still holding the protesting bird, and began beating it against the solid ground like a dusty old rug, swearing with every strike. When the creature went limp in her grip, she dashed it against the wall.

The Kauroch raised itself off of Padre, and the man took a much needed but painful breath. Padre tried to crawl to freedom. But the Kauroch struck again, not with its body, but by driving its beak through Padre's back. His spinal column broke in the process. Gunfire erupted, and the beast turned its wrath on the shooters, leaving Padre to his fate.

Alyssa slid to kneel at Padre's side. She examined the wound to find that the beak had gone clear through his body. His cheek rested against the ice, blank eyes staring through raspy breaths. "Goddamnit, Padre. Who am I supposed to argue theology with now?" she joked, managing to keep the merriment in her eyes for Padre's sake.

"We never argued," Padre said through ragged breaths. "Saying we argued would imply...equal knowledge. You lack a foundation from which...to argue the most basic points."

Alyssa shook her head and couldn't help but laugh. She saw the corner of Padre's mouth raise. "Well I hope you won our debates and you're right about your God," she said leaning near his face.

Padre couldn't see her but he felt the warmth of her skin near his. "Me too," he said in a whisper.

A-Bomb felt more than heard the penguins coming up behind her. She pivoted into a leg sweep and toppled the four would-be killers over. She stood and stomped on the birds, like an angry chef stamping out cockroaches in a greasy kitchen. The penguins tried to scatter, but her boots found the first two penguin's heads and the third, a larger Adélie, she stomped on thrice to render it immobile. The fourth, a Southern Rockhopper, tried to scoot away on its stomach, but A-Bomb's boot found the birds foot. The Rockhopper screeched in protest until she plucked it up by it's head and twirled the hapless bird like a lasso, nearly wrenching its head from its body.

A-Bomb looked for her M4 automatic rifle but couldn't find it. She scanned the ground dumbfounded by the guns disappearance. She looked for Padre's weapon, but it too was gone. She spun in a circle trying to find anybody's gun. Ten or more men had already died, there had to be one lying amongst the carnage. Then she spotted the culprit—an Adélie that was missing half of one wing was dragging a rifle by the strap, headed for the ice-hole. "Hey," she shouted. The penguin deposited the gun in the water.

A-Bomb took a few steps toward the thief, but it quickly fled into the alcove. "Shit," was all she could muster. She looked for a weapon and found one: the Warlord's pike. She snatched up the spear and spotted Talus braining a wounded man in the wake of the Kauroch's rampage. The Warlord had put the Kauroch between him and surviving squad members. She marched forward, intent on ending the freakish penguin's life.

CHAPTER 15

General Talus marveled at the havoc just one Kauroch could wreak. If he had just a few more, this fight would've been over. He briefly entertained calling the chariot, but the battle was too pitched for him to get away to unfasten the harnesses. Berating himself over the decision to leave one Kauroch out of the fray, he was still having as grand a time as he had ever had. Spotting a human near his feet, cast aside by the Kauroch, Talus bashed the prone man on the head.

The smaller penguins disengaged their opponents to make room for the Kauroch. The huge beast, blinded by rage, attacked everything in its path. It slapped with gull wings as it clawed forward with great speed. The humans were forced to turn and run, but even that couldn't save some from the monster's wrath. It raked its deadly beak through flesh like a plow through soft soil. The humans fired. The Kauroch bellowed with fury and kept charging through the hail of bullets until it finally fell, exhaling a mighty last breath.

The smaller penguins who had taken cover behind the beast charged forward, attacking the first human they came to en masse. The man fired his gun into the throng, but a few Rockhoppers made it through the carnage. They leapt at the man, making him fall backwards while still firing. The bullets tore through the body of another man, and a third human dove for cover.

Talus took delight in seeing the human kill one of his own. "I believe the humans have an expression, 'killing two birds with one stone.' The stone is certainly in the other nest now," he said. He stepped forward, fully intent on destruction, when he heard the footfalls of a human coming at him from behind. Talus turned and screeched an unholy sound.

A-Bomb didn't flinch. She fixed her spear at her target with a jouster's accuracy. The Warlord swung his club to meet her lunge, deflecting the pike with a swift swipe. He followed up with a backhanded swing of his club that she had to lean back to avoid. Blood and bits of scalp from the Warlord's previous victims sprayed across her face.

A-Bomb planted her feet, and using the pike as a staff, swung and struck the Warlord across the side of the head. She brought it back across for another hit.

The Warlord remained on his feet, rage burning in his eyes. He was furious at being struck by his own weapon, but kept the fury under control. He brought the heft of his club down on the woman, who brought the pike up in a two-handed block. The pike snapped in half, and A-Bomb fell to her backside.

"Oh shit," A-Bomb yelped, seeing the penguin's unexpected strength.

"Oh sshhit, indeed human," Talus was uncertain of the meaning of the word, but he was sure of its vulgarity. He struck again, narrowly missing her face. He watched her scurry to her feet, deftly evading each consecutive strike. Talus was unrelenting. Blow after blow rained down at her, and each was avoided or deflected away with the broken pike she carried in each hand.

A-Bomb dodged until she found an opening. She ducked beneath a wild swing, then brought the piece of wood down on the Warlord's head like a billy club. She spun in with a back-handed strike of the sharp end of the pike, and plunged it into Talus' body.

The shock of pain sent adrenaline through Talus' body. Never had he met such an opponent. He could recall only once when anything had struck such a blow. He looked at the offending bit of wood and was once again thankful for Cryzyrky's foresight. The tip had only slightly broken through the thick seal leather. Talus shifted his body and pinned A-Bomb's arm beneath his flipper, keeping her close. He leaned his face close to the woman. "That hurt," he said and brought his club down on her arm with enough force to shatter bone.

A-Bomb screamed out in agony and fell to the ground. Her left forearm was shattered, and she could feel the bone protruding through the flesh. The mad penguin brought his club down again and just missed her leg. She regained her wits and clambered to her feet. She had to get away. She turned and ran, clutching her useless left arm against her body.

"And I thought this one would be a worthy opponent," Talus said, giving chase. The thrill of pursuing his prey was delightful. He felt as if he were swimming through the sea in pursuit of a particularly evasive fish. But this fish fought back, more like a Leopard Seal. He would have to use a bit of caution while hunting this game, even if he had wounded it.

A-Bomb fell against the west wall of the outpost. The pain in her arm was nearly unbearable. She struggled to remove her pack, watching the Warlord run toward her all the while. She fought with the zipper, her last resort lying on the other side of interlocking metal teeth. She swore and tore at the zipper, which began to budge. She reached for flare gun inside, but it was too late. The Warlord was there. She rolled to her right and the club met the frozen wall where her head had been just a moment before. She jumped to her feet, every move sending jolts of pain through her arm.

Talus stood before A-Bomb, a lust for killing burning in his eyes. "Where were we before you chose to flee? Oh yes, I was about to kill you," he said through a hiss.

Though surprised by the bird's command of the language, she didn't let on. "I think it's my turn now," she said defiantly. Talus hissed and attacked. Each swing of his club came close, but A-Bomb dodged every strike. She had studied him enough now to know that his strength lay in lateral strikes, and overhead attacks were much slower and appeared awkward for the penguin. Talus roared, becoming frustrated by the human's agility. A-Bomb met his cry with a spinning round-house kick that knocked the Warlord to the ground in a blink.

Talus forced his eyes open. That was a good hit, he thought. As much as he admired the woman's fight, he had to do something quick or he would find out if the Ancients truly existed very soon. He looked for his weapon. Spotting it several meters away, he scooted himself toward his equalizer. A heavy booted kick to his mid-section sent him spinning across the ice. The world became a haze of confusion. This human, not as large as the others he had already killed, put up more of fight than he had ever experienced. Perhaps it was a different species, bred to compensate for its lack of size with ferocious cunning and agility. Whatever it was, he had to do something to turn the tides.

Talus recited a silent offering to the Ancients, desperately seeking salvation. He didn't fear dying so much as he feared losing a fight. He opened his eyes and saw the human warrior walking toward him confidently, despite clutching her damaged arm to her side. He looked the other way and caught sight of his gift. By a miracle bestowed on him by the Ancients, the club was within reach. He took it in his grasp as he felt the vibrations of the warrior. She was running the final distance to attack again. Talus lay still and his eyes smiled in satisfaction. Now he would end this fight.

As A-Bomb stepped and brought her right foot up to deliver a crushing blow to the Warlord's skull, Talus flipped over, brought the club around, and met the side of her knee. The force of the hit sent A-Bomb to the ground. Talus pushed himself up and looked over his opponent. He had dealt another wound, but would it be enough to slow this creature down? He gave it the chance to stand and let out a satisfied guttural click at seeing her fall back to one knee. It was time to kill this one.

Talus swung hard, catching A-Bomb on the left shoulder, sending currents of pain through her broken arm. He brought the club back from the follow through and caught her on the right shoulder. Back and forth, left side and right side, he beat A-Bomb viciously.

A-Bomb could do nothing. The strikes came so fast, all she could was turn with each blow to deflect the energy. The next hit struck her on the left side, and she knew immediately that her ribs had been broken. She nearly fell, but Talus took her by her coat and pulled her up. "No, not yet," he said. "You need to stay awake for this."

A-Bomb looked at the Warlord in confusion. Whether it was the delirium from the pain or lack of oxygen at not from the broken ribs, she wasn't sure. Why did she need to stay awake when all she wanted to do was lay down? Her unspoken question was answered a moment later.

Talus swung again and struck A-Bomb across the side of her head with his club. She fell in a crumpled heap on the ice. Gouts of blood dripped down her face faster than the freezing air could coagulate the flow. The Warlord stood over Alyssa, watching the pool of crimson expand on the icy white canvas. He marveled at the work of art he had created and looked at his weapon. Sticky with blood, he admired the tufts of hair and fabric trapped in the gore. "This truly is a weapon of the Ancients," he said in awe. He surveyed the arena and saw one man standing, fending off two Royal Emperors and a handful of the smaller races. The day belonged to Talus; this battle would soon be over. Confident that the Ancients were truly at his side, he strode forward to send this human to his maker.

CHAPTER 16

Trofim saw Alyssa fall in the waning daylight. He wanted nothing more than to run to her, to carry her out of this unimaginable hell they were in and get her to a field hospital. He wasn't going to let Alyssa die…if she hadn't already. But he had more than a few obstacles to clear before he got to the business of saving her. While Alyssa had been engaged in a life and death duel with the Big Bastard, as Tro had come to think of him, two Royals and a handful of other penguins seemed to be intent on killing him. Or, at the very least, they were keeping him occupied until the Big Bastard arrived to finish the task.

Though he was approaching exhaustion from the intense, non-stop, personal combat, amplified by the extreme cold, he still had a fire in him. That fire had been stoked at seeing Alyssa fall. All he needed was a gun and this would be over in seconds. Another thought entered his mind as he twisted the spear out of a Royal's grip, turned the crude weapon on its former owner, and pierced the steroidal looking penguin through its chest. With Alyssa down, impossibly, he was the last man standing, and her only hope of salvation.

As he pulled the spear from the first one's torso, letting it fall before him, the second Royal slapped Trofim across the face with its surprisingly strong flipper. He backhanded the slapper across its face. Feeling the steel coated beak rip through his glove and open a gash on his hand, he immediately regretted the choice. But the backhanded blow was enough to knock the oversized bird off balance, giving him a chance to deal with the more diminutive sort that were doing their best to separate his calf from his leg.

He stomped out the life of the one causing him the most trouble. He found room to step back and deliver a kick to the next that would have made his dead commander proud. But three kills in less than a minute only put a *dent in the bucket*, as he so often inaccurately put it. The smaller penguins were replaced by three more, and to make matters worse he noticed that the Big Bastard had turned his attention toward him.

Trofim looked around and finally spotted a gun—a Mossberg 500 shotgun lying in what he thought of as the latrine about four meters away. The weapon had belonged to Fob, and how it had ended up so far from where the man had died, he hadn't a clue. He made a move toward the gun, but was met by the other Royal. Tro drove his elbow into the penguin's throat, dropping the avian once again. A stab in his already bloodied calf made him wince, but didn't slow him. Taking two long strides, he dove the remaining distance and slid through the acrid muck, grabbing the shotgun as he slid past it. He hoped the weapon wasn't empty. He shucked the forend while lying on his back. He took aim at the crowd of penguins in pursuit.

The first blast leveled the first two attackers, and the second and third shots took care of the rest. He fired another round at the approaching Big Bastard, but it was still too far out of the gun's effective range. It was enough to give the creature pause as the pellets that found their target and peppered his leather armor. He prepared to fire another shot at a lower angle, to hopefully have a few pellets hit its unprotected legs, but he was struck hard across the face by the staff of the Royal he thought he killed with the elbow strike. He reflexively squeezed the trigger, wasting the precious round on the corpse of the Kauroch.

Trofim rolled out of the way of next attack, a stabbing thrust that would have impaled him had he not had the presence of mind to move. Why the penguin didn't lead with the stab was beyond him. Maybe they enjoyed punishing their prey before they killed it. Or maybe they were arrogant with delusions of superiority. God knew he had seen enough men during his time in combat to know that might be the case. It gave them a sense of control when the world around them spun hopelessly into chaos. Whatever the reason might have been, the penguin was about to pay for its lack of foresight. He pumped the shot-gun, seeing the discharged empty shell spin through the ever fading light from the edge of his vision, and fired.

The penguin howled when its flipper tore away from its body. Not satisfied with wounding the animal, Trofim stood and fired again. The penguin's head scattered in a hundred different directions at once and the remnants of its body fell away. Tro looked for another nearby target, but found none. They were all dead, all except for that Big Bastard. He took inventory of his wounds. There were plenty, that he knew, but none were immediately life-threatening. He inhaled deeply, not caring about the icy burn of the cold air, and rotated his head down and around to loosen stiff muscles. There was one more obstacle to overcome before he could get to Alyssa.

CHAPTER 17

Talus watched Trofim kill all of his attackers, admiring the man's ability in combat. Each move had been efficient and deadly, with only the mistake of focusing too much on him, which should have cost the man his life. No matter how Talus had tried to scrub out the Royal's cocksure attitude, he hadn't completely wiped away years of training under the bloated half-wit, Liutites. However confident Talus may have been after defeating A-Bomb, he was hesitant to move closer to the last human after feeling the sting of the buckshot.

Talus moved a little but stopped. He wasn't afraid of death, but he wasn't so filled with bravado as to walk straight into death's waiting jaws. He tried to figure a way to even the odds. The man had a gun and all he had was a club. While he appreciated Cryzryky disposing of the human weapons, he would have like to have found out how to use one—they were so efficient at dealing death. He considered diving into the seal hole and waiting the human out, but the seal skin leather would likely weight him down to the point of drowning him. His internal deliberations ended when he saw the man boldly walking toward him. The Warlord let out a heavy breath and matched the human's bold walk.

Trofim and Talus stopped their bold walking and faced one another with just two meters separating them. "You have fought well, human. You are a true warrior among your kind, and it appears as though the Ancients have found you victorious. I commend you on your victory, for no creature has bested me in combat," Talus said. He resigned himself to defeat. His options were played out, and it seemed as though the Ancients were at last calling him to The Great Sea. He uttered a barely audible warble to Cryzyrky to let her know that now was the time for her to go.

Trofim stared at Talus. He marveled at the penguin's speaking ability. Though it sounded a bit parrot-like, but with a deeper tone, it was the most impressive show of intelligence in a creature he had come across. He doubted what he was about to do. The protocols said to create a dialogue; he should capture it and bring it in for study. But he decided to hell with protocols; this son-of-a-bitch had killed Alyssa and several others.

Trofim studied the penguin a moment longer and decided to find out what he could before he blew its head off. "Before I kill you," he said, leveling the gun at the Warlord's head, "tell me why you're doing this. Why is your kind attacking us?"

After he said he said it, he realized it sounded rather lame and a bit desperate, more in tune with pleading for an answer, and in a way it was true. There seemed to be something more going on than what he knew and he had to make sense of it all.

Talus hissed a laugh. "Why I am doing this? I am doing this because I enjoy killing, I enjoy the sport of it. It is why the Ancients brought me into this world, simply to kill—not the weak and helpless; where is the challenge in killing a fledgling? But to test my strength against strength, so that I may find my place at their side and give strength to those who may follow me in life and in death. As for the attacks you refer to, why, your kind has been killing ours for generations. I believe a little payback was in order. Myself, I don't care for revenge. It upsets the gullet. Revenge and drawn out campaigns are the doings of the Overlord. He desires an empire, and to rule as his ancestors did." Talus deliberately put more questions into the man's head. If he could keep him talking long enough, he might be able to get close enough to attack. He took a step forward.

This was news. An Overlord? Judging by the penguin's size and apparent authority, Trofim had guessed that this was leader of the penguins. Whatever the Overlord was, Tro guessed that this one had no love for it, and thought that he might be able to pry more information out. But he would have to do it quickly, if he was to save Alyssa. He lowered the gun slightly and Talus took another step which brought the weapon back up. "Who or what is this *overlord*? And where can I find it?"

Talus took another small step and Trofim tensed making the Warlord stop again. "The Overlord is what the title implies," Talus answered, inching a little closer. "A creature as intelligent as you appear to be should know that. As far as where…well, perhaps you should ask the right human." Talus saw Trofim's head tilt ever so slightly with suspicion. He had him. The human's curiosity had been piqued. He took another step and saw Trofim take a small step backwards. To Talus, the step meant that the human wasn't ready to kill him just yet.

"Who are you talking about, what human?" Trofim thought it had to be Colonel Jenson. But why wouldn't the colonel just go in a blast them all to hell? No, there was somebody else. The metal tipped beaks were a sure sign that this overlord had been in league with somebody. But who and why? No, it wasn't Jenson. He was looking for the Overlord. Millerton had mentioned something about getting information. Lyons—that was the name. He had to find the man named Lyons.

"How am I supposed to know who?" Talus asked, taking another step that was matched by Trofim's backward step. He gripped his club tightly. The time to strike would come soon. "You humans are such a motley set. Each face so different from another. Like stones on the shore; everyone is different, but together they are just a pile of rocks. In truth, I never saw the human. And the one penguin here that had, you had the courtesy to remove his head with your weapon not moments ago," Talus said, taking another step and indicating the dead Royal Trofim had just killed. "It's a shame that the dead can't give you answers."

Trofim guessed that this penguin was stalling and any information he had could be found be found by other means. Time was running out for Alyssa, if it hadn't already. These things were smart, and Trofim was certain that there were any number of them that could give him the same answers, or be coerced into telling him more. If Millerton hadn't killed the Chinstrap, he might have gotten those answers. "True, the dead don't give up their secrets. And apparently, neither do the living." Trofim braced the kick of the shotgun and pulled the trigger. The click was followed by an unexpected silence. Trofim began to curse someone's mother, but the Warlord's attack wouldn't allow him to complete the expletive.

Trofim brought the empty shotgun up to block the Warlord's blow. Wood met steel and plastic and shattered the forend instead of Trofim's skull. Tro weakly swung the gun at the penguin's head, not having the time for a proper swipe. The Warlord swung again, this time catching him on his right shoulder. It hurt, but pain was an extraneous feeling now. Tro turned and caught the Warlord's flipper in his hand as he swung again. The bird's strength caught him by surprise, and he had to struggle to push the flipper away.

Talus struggled to pull his wing away from Trofim, but couldn't break loose. He brought his other up to slap the man away, but the man caught it. He now had both flippers stuck in the man's iron grip. Unable to break free, the Warlord stabbed his beak into Trofim's chest, causing him to loosen his grip. His relief was momentary; he was struck by a right cross to head. Talus stumbled back and was met by another hard punch. He brought his club up to counter, but was met with a third blow.

Trofim reared back to deliver the knockout punch with another hard right, but Talus swung his club. All he could do was bring his left arm up to block. Fortunately for Trofim, the Warlord's strike was defensive and lacked the power of a full strike. The bash hurt, but it wasn't enough to break bone. Talus followed up with a backhanded swing powerful enough, that if Trofim hadn't pulled his head back, the fight would have ended right then and there. As it was, the club nicked Trofim on the forehead. He stumbled back and lost his footing. He landed hard on his back and threw himself into a backward somersault, giving him distance on the advancing Warlord.

Talus charged in quickly and Trofim delivered a kick to his gut. It was now the Warlord's turn to lie on his back. Trofim was quick to his feet, and rushed to take advantage of the turn of events. Tro reached for the Warlord's throat, hoping to snap his neck, but instead he received a stunning blow to the side of his head, which sent him rolling off of his enemy.

Both combatants got to their feet and faced off once more. Talus swung his club back and forth, driving his opponent back and not giving him an opening to counter. Trofim stepped back, drawing the Warlord to him. He had to find a way to get that accursed club away from the creature and end this fight now. He reached for his knife, but found it gone. When and where had he dropped it? He stepped back once more, and his foot found the edge of the seal hole. Trofim teetered on the edge of losing his balance. If he fell in, he would freeze to death in minutes if not sooner.

Talus swung again, hoping to send the man to meet his maker in the icy depths. He had to finish this fight soon. The long day of combat was draining his strength, and he felt the burn of exhaustion with every missed strike. The swinging club failed to meet its target, and the man dove to his left, and away from the hole. Frustration began to eat at the Warlord's resolve. He turned to face Trofim with his mouth agape, sucking in the cold air to replenish tired muscles.

Trofim got to one knee. He too was tired, muscles aching with fatigue. The ridiculous cold was taking its toll, and for the first time he began to doubt the outcome. He saw the Warlord standing with his beak open, staring at him. He knew it wasn't awe the penguin was looking at him with; the creature was approaching exhaustion. Both of them wanted nothing more than for the fight to be over, but neither willing to concede defeat.

Talus clenched his beak firmly, and on heavy legs, moved toward his opponent again. This time he would be done with it, one way or another. He drew his club back to swing, hoping to brain the man once and for all.

Trofim stood to face the attack. Seeing the Warlord rear back to strike, he planted his left foot and delivered a round house kick to his adversary's side, knocking him back but not down. The pain from the torn flesh in his calf faltered him, and his leg gave out mid-strike, causing him to collapse to the ground. He didn't think it was possible to sweat in this cold, but he felt like he was. The Warlord came at him again and he blocked the attack, countering with a punch to Talus' side from his knees.

Talus let out a grunt as the man's rock-like fist caught him in the ribs. Layers of fat and the leather garb deflected the full impact, but it was enough to make his exhausted legs wobble. He switched the club to his other hand, no longer trusting the other to hold the weight of the heavy piece of lumber. He stumbled in to attempt another attack, and took another punch from Trofim's left. The man was tiring, but so was Talus. He just had to outlast him, that's all that was required. Talus came in again, but seeing the man prepare to block the club, he brought his right flipper in and slapped Trofim hard across the face.

The slap was hard enough to stun Trofim, sending shock waves of pain through his head. In the next moment, Talus brought his club around. All Tro could do was cover his head. Wood met skull bone and Trofim slumped to his side. Had it been earlier in the day, before the weariness of battle sapped the Big Bastard's strength, the club would have split his head open. He looked up and saw stars that had nothing to with the approaching night. This was it, Tro thought. Bested by a goddamned bird.

Talus stood over Trofim, watching him try to push himself up on rubbery arms, only to fall again. The thrill of victory elicited a burst of energy and reinvigorated his fight. "Now, human. I will finish this."

CHAPTER 18

Alyssa opened one eye, her other shut by frozen blood. She pressed her shoulder against the impossibly cold ground and lifted her head. The throbbing pain was tremendous but she pushed herself up, resisting the urge to vomit as waves of concussive nausea rolled through her body. Her vision was muddied, and the daylight was disappearing into the dark polar night, making her strain to see anything at all. She flexed her right hand but didn't bother with the left, the pain giving her total recall of the damage she had sustained. She felt like regurgitated death, but at least she wasn't actually dead.

Through the faint light and glow of the white sheet of ice, scarred by the blood and corpses of the fallen, Alyssa spotted the movement. There were two figures dancing in the shadows on the far side of the ice hole. It took a moment for her to register what she was seeing. It was not the forms of lovers stealing away in a darkened courtyard, as her mind first told her it was, but a man and creature engaged in fierce combat. Through her clouded mind, she recognized the shape of the man and she managed a smile. It was Trofim. Of course it was. If any of them were to have survived the unexpected ferocity of this day, he was the most likely candidate.

With one almost good arm and an equally almost good leg, Alyssa pushed herself to her feet. The world spun around her, and this time she couldn't hold her stomach contents in. She fell back to the ground, waiting for heaving spasms to cease. They call me the A-Bomb, she reminded herself. She forced herself up again. Even though her surroundings spun around like children dancing in a circle, devilishly taunting another child on the playground, she found her strength and remained on her feet. "That's right," she said in a hoarse whisper. "Who do they call A-Bomb? Me. That's right." She smiled inwardly and limped forward.

A-Bomb watched the fight between Trofim and the Warlord at a distance, not wanting to distract Tro from his work. Every time it seemed as though either one was getting the upper hand, the other would equalize the fight in some manner. A thought occurred to her. What if Trofim couldn't win this fight? What if he had been injured? It was the only reason she could think of as to why he hadn't already killed the bastard. Feeling suddenly vulnerable, she scanned her surroundings trying to find something for protection…anything. She found it in the form of the Warlord's broken pike. She picked up the splintered spear-tip and examined the pointed end. This would do. It would have to do. She could find nothing else. That pain in the ass little penguin with the missing flipper had seen to that.

She looked back at the raging fight. Both combatants looked as if they were about to fall over with exhaustion. Her heart skipped a beat when she realized Trofim was down on one knee. She saw him punch the penguin in the side, he was holding his own in the fight, but she knew he was in trouble. A-Bomb clenched the broken pike in her good hand and limped forward. It was time to turn the odds in Trofim's favor. The abbreviated day had been long enough, and the night would longer if they didn't get out of there soon.

Pushing and willing herself forward and around the hole, she saw Trofim go down. The penguin had somehow managed to do what a hundred other things and a thousand men hadn't been able to. It beat him. She watched the penguin stand in front of Trofim, wobbly on its feet, but triumphant in stature. She willed her legs to carry her the five meters separating them. She pushed harder. Three meters to go. She urged what remained of her strength and raised the broken pike above her like a dagger. One more meter and this all would be over with.

A-Bomb heard what sounded to her like the bleating of a sheep coming from her right. The noise pulled her eyes away from her target for less than a second, and when she returned her attention to Talus, she caught sight of the broad end of the club just before it stuck her in her face. She had braced herself in that fraction of a second before impact and for the extreme pain to be followed by darkness. But the pain and darkness didn't come. Instead, everything turned bright white and the pain was more of a dull yet somehow intense ache. For a brief moment she felt like she was in flight, floating on a cushion of clouds. The sensation was simultaneously comforting, yet frightening. Then she felt the impact of her back slamming against ice. The cloud disappeared, but strangely her head was still floating. A dozen cherished memories swam though her mind. Walking on the warm sand of a beach near her home with her father, traveling the world and lovers she had long forgotten; happy times and heartache flooded her mind followed by visions of things that would never come to pass. A man yelling at a ballgame on the radio and his smile as she walked out the door holding a jar of kvass. The feeling of those thoughts and memories warmed her even as the icy stab of the Antarctic water pierced her head. She slid deeper into water so cold that it burned. She was floating again, but not on cushioned cloud. This time it was a bed of nails, no, not nails, but a mattress of daggers. Then finally the darkness came and the knives disappeared.

CHAPTER 19

Trofim lifted his head, trying to shake out cobwebs that had ensnared his thoughts. He saw Talus standing over him, almost as if he were gloating. And judging by the penguin's disposition, it likely was. And then he saw Alyssa and he smiled. She was alive and she was going to kill the Big Bastard. Then he heard what he thought was a sheep. How the hell did a sheep get out here? And then he realized it was the bleating call of an Adélie penguin. It was a warning, and Talus had turned so quickly with club in hand that Trofim didn't have time to shout out his own warning.

Horror punched Trofim in gut when he saw Alyssa slide into the water. There would be no saving her. Even if he could pull her out, without immediate evac she would die within minutes. And there was the Bastard to deal with. He felt the rage course through his body. The unfamiliar feeling of helplessness at seeing Alyssa die ignited his last reserve of energy. He had to get to her.

The Warlord turned back toward his next kill just as Trofim got to his feet. He brought his weapon up to strike again, but he knew that only the will of the Ancients would prevent him from dying this time.

Trofim took two quick steps leapt in the air and drop kicked Talus across the ice. He knew it was a disabling blow and didn't bother to follow up. All that mattered now was pulling Alyssa from the water before she sank out of reach. He crawled on his stomach to the brink of the hole, feeling the freshly formed ice along the edges crack beneath his weight. He didn't care; he only cared about pulling Alyssa from the deadly water. He reached out, stretching his arm as far as he could and caught by her collar. He tugged with his last bit of strength and pulled her out of the void.

Trofim held Alyssa's body close, wrapping his arms around as tight as he could, willing her to stay alive. He could give a damn about the water soaking through the rents in his clothing. He spoke to her softly, with his face pressed against hers, the redness of his cheeks lying against the blueness of hers. He urged her to stay with him, but no amount of begging and pleading could bring her back from where she had gone. Trofim's body began to quiver. He heard the thumping of helicopter blades in the distance, striking the wind in cadence with his sobs. The evac was finally coming, but it was too late. There had been so many who died today, people he had known for a decade or more. He wondered why Alyssa's death had impacted him so hard. Was it the stress? Was it the frustration of being unable to quickly defeat such a primitive enemy? And he knew why. She had loved baseball too, and however unlikely it might have been, they would never sit together on a porch and listen to a game. His future, like the past, was gone.

CHAPTER 20

Talus lay on the ice for a full minute before trying to stand. The Ancients had indeed been with him. The human had kicked him with such fury that the blow had sent him flailing across the ice. He had skirted the edge of the seal hole, missing the plunge by mere inches. The weight of the leather would have pulled him to the sea floor, and in his weakened state there would have been little he could do about such a fate. But the Ancients had intervened once again, and his life was spared.

He stood slowly and looked for his weapon. He spotted it floating on the surface of the water, as symbolically out of reach as a victory was today—so close, but in the end unattainable. He saw Trofim holding his comrade, weeping. He considered going to him and driving his beak through the back of the man's neck, but thought better of it. Talus, for the first time in his life, had been defeated. The sound of approaching flying machines dispersed any lingering doubt about what course of action he should take. He had survived the day and he would live to fight again. He gave the man and his dead compatriot an admiring look—true warriors they were.

He walked on weak legs to Forward Command's exit. "Let's go, Cryzyrky. There are more on the way." Cryzyrky didn't say a word as she came out of the alcove and followed the Warlord out.

Once outside, Talus was surprised to find the Kauroch with its chariot waiting close by. He climbed up the ramp at the rear and Cryzyrky dutifully followed. "That was good thinking to bring the Kauroch to us," he said, ever impressed by the Adélie's foresight.

"I guessed that *we* would be needing to make a quick escape," she said, basking in the glow of his praise.

"What would I do without you, my friend?" he said, with a warmth that she, or in fact no other penguin had ever heard him intonate.

"Probably what I would do without you, General," she said, still playfully mocking his appointed title.

"And what would that be?"

"Die," Cryzyrky said with all seriousness, but with a hint of affection which told Talus all he needed to know.

Talus looked at her for several seconds, appraising her, the moment and the entire day. "No truer words have ever been spoken, my friend," he finally said. He urged the Kauroch forward and they sped off into the darkness, leaving Forward Command and the war to the Overlord.

CHAPTER 21

The low flying helicopters flew over Forward Command, and sent whirlwinds of pinfeathers into the night sky. Spotlights circled the perimeter searching for what they could, finally coming to rest on Trofim sitting on the ground, still clinging to Alyssa. Trofim shielded his eyes and weakly gave a small wave to indicate he was alive. He stood and gently pried Alyssa's body away, the water having frozen her clothing to his.

Two choppers landed behind the outpost while one remained circling above, scanning the ground for any potential threat. Tro stiffly walked around the compound and spotted the glint of his knife lying amongst a gathering of dead birds. A spotlight shined through the opening at the back of the outpost, silhouetting the form of man. Trofim ignored the man even as he approached.

"Soldier," the man said.

Trofim decided he didn't like the man from his first word and continued to ignore him.

"Soldier, I am speaking to you," said the man, with a bit more command in his voice.

Trofim held his knife at his side and looked at the man, unable to make out his features from blinding light behind him. "Yes?"

"That's yes sir," the man said.

Now Trofim knew he didn't like him. "Yes sir?" he said, inflecting as much attitude as his Russian accent would allow.

The man looked him over, observing the various wounds that were visible through his gear. "What's your name?"

"Sergeant Trofim Aleksandr Grekov, sir," Tro said completely devoid of emotion.

"Are you the only one left?"

Tro looked at Alyssa's body, stiff in her carapace of frozen clothing. "Yessir."

The man nodded and looked around the courtyard. "Did any of the indigenous species survive?"

Trofim looked around for the body of Talus and couldn't find it. The Big Bastard had escaped while he wasn't looking. He thought about it. He was nearly incapacitated. Not nearly; he had been completely incapacitated while holding Alyssa, and yet the penguin didn't kill him. He wondered why. Maybe it was as fatigued as he was, or had fallen into the water, or maybe it had its own reasons. Whatever the reasons, it hadn't killed him when it easily could have. Trofim would not be so forgiving if he ever encountered the thing again. Trofim looked at the man. "No sir. No penguins survived."

"Well done," the man said, though Tro didn't feel any sincerity in his praise. "Get yourself to the chopper and clear out. I'll see to the clean-up."

Trofim nodded. He looked at Alyssa one last time and started to walk away. He stopped and looked back at the man.

"Yes, soldier?" the man asked.

"I'll be needing to speak to you very soon...Colonel Jenson." Trofim turned and walked to the helicopter. He was certain of it now—he really didn't like him.

More from Rockhopper Books

Rise of the Penguins Saga

Rise of the Penguins
Book 1

Crosscurrents
Book 3

Whispers of Shadows
Book 4

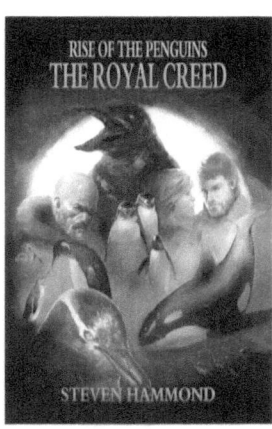

The Royal Creed
Book 5

Order of Kings
Book 6

The Great Auk War
Book 7
(coming soon)